OUR SNOWMAN HAD OLIVE EYES

by CHARLOTTE HERMAN

OUR SNOWMAN HAD OLIVE EYES

by CHARLOTTE HERMAN

cover illustration by Gloria Kamen

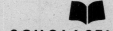

SCHOLASTIC INC.

NEW YORK · TORONTO · LONDON · AUCKLAND · SYDNEY · TOKYO

In memory
of my Bubbies,
Chana and Rivka

ISBN 0-590-30253-1

12 11 10 9 8 7 6 5 4   4 5 6 7/8

One

Bubbie's teeth are sitting on the window sill. They're just sitting there staring at me through a glass of Efferdent. Her teeth are the first thing I see when I wake up in the morning and the last thing I see before I go to bed at night. I wish she'd stick them behind the window curtain so I wouldn't have to look at them all the time. But I wouldn't think of telling her to do that. I try not to hurt her feelings.

Bubbie is my grandma. She lives with us now. Before she came here she lived alone in a small apartment building with three floors. Every Saturday my mother, my sister Muriel, and I would walk the six blocks to visit her. I got to play with Myron who lived on the third floor, and eat Eskimo Pies that the grocer gave us — for free — because he liked Bubbie. And sometimes I even got to sleep overnight on the davenport. Bubbie calls it a davenport. I call it a couch.

1

Then one Sunday at breakfast Mother announced, "Bubbie is coming to live with us. It's been hard for her to get around lately and she needs someone to look after her. Well, she's getting old, you know." Bubbie's old? Of course she's old. What's new about that? I don't ever remember her looking young. She's always had gray hair and wrinkles on her face.

"But she's always been old," I said. "So how come she's moving in all of a sudden?"

"She wasn't always old," Mother said. "She just looked that way. Because of her life. She worked hard raising seven children all alone when your grandpa, your Zayde, died, and worrying about us all the time. Lots of worry can make a young person look old."

"But moving in! No more Saturday walks. No more Myron. No more Eskimo Pies. And no more davenport."

"Silly," said Muriel, as she attacked a second helping of wheat cakes. "We have a davenport right in our living room."

"That's a couch," I said.

Daddy stirred an extra teaspoon of sugar in his coffee. "You'll like having Bubbie living here with us. Even I will. She's easy to get along with."

"Sidney, watch the sugar. Remember your diet," Mother said, taking a sip of her own black, sugarless coffee. Ugh!

"But where will she sleep?" I asked, thinking of our three bedrooms already occupied.

2

"We were thinking of having Bubbie share your room, Sheila."

"My room?" I screamed. "Why my room? We just moved to this house. I just got my room. I've waited ten years for a room of my own. What about Muriel?"

"Well, I've waited fifteen years for mine," Muriel shouted at me. "Besides, I don't think Bubbie would like my decor."

Muriel's room looks like Democratic Headquarters. She's got pictures of Democratic presidents, senators, and all sorts of big-shot politicians plastered on all the walls of her bedroom.

I have some pictures on my walls too, but not nearly as many as Muriel does. Just a few sketches of Famous Composers — Bach, Mozart, and Beethoven — that my mother gave me when I started taking piano lessons.

"I don't see how even you can like your decor," I said to Muriel. "Doesn't it make you feel creepy with all those faces staring at you all the time?"

"Not in the least," she said. "It's quiet company."

"We really ought to put the two of you together," Daddy suggested. "That way Bubbie can have her own room. It would be best for her."

"You mean *us* together!" Muriel complained. "Her and me? Never again. I need my privacy."

"Yeah, that's what I figured you'd say," said Daddy.

Muriel needs her privacy. Ha. She sits locked up in her room all day, reading books — nonfiction ones — and magazines and writing in her private journal.

Mother and Daddy say she'll probably become a writer one day. But I know different. I read her private journal all the time. Or at least I used to. Up until a short while ago. Muriel has no imagination. She writes things like:

8:15 a.m. We had scrambled eggs for breakfast.
1:00 p.m. It's raining out.
4:00 p.m. I just noticed. My library book is overdue.
9:00 p.m. Time for bed. Good night.

Now how can anyone who writes a journal like that become a writer? And she has no imagination in other ways too. Once when we were on the way to the library I stopped to look up at the sky, and I saw two goats being chased by a witch. "Oh, Muriel," I said. "Look up at the sky and tell me what you see."

So she looked up and said, "Clouds. Come on, we're late."

"I guess it's settled then," Mother said to me. "Bubbie will stay in your room."

Muriel grinned. And that got me mad.

"You always side with her!"

"Don't take it so hard," Daddy said. "If it doesn't work out, Bubbie can always share a room with your mother and me." And he sat there tilting his chair back and laughing. I wasn't in the mood to listen to him, so I jumped away from the table and left Muriel there to help with the dishes.

I put my jacket on and went out into the autumn air to Rita's house. Rita lives a block and a half away, right next to where I used to live when we had the two-bedroom house. Every time Rita spent the night we had to sleep on the floor in the living room. But I always promised her, "When we move I'll get my own room with an extra bed and you'll sleep over all the time and it'll be great."

Then just about a year ago we moved, and I got my room and Rita came over a lot and slept in the extra bed — the one by the door.

As I was walking, I thought about Bubbie coming to live with us and wondered what it would be like having her share my room. I don't think I really minded it. She *is* easy to get along with. Just like Daddy said. She's quiet and kind and she's always doing nice things for me, like giving me too much to eat whenever I came over. She's not bossy like Rita's grandmother. Rita doesn't get along with her grandmother. She calls her a witch.

I think what really bothered me most was the idea that Muriel was getting her way again. Like when we first moved in, Muriel was given first choice in picking out a bedroom. So of course she picked the larger room. Actually, I don't really care. My bedroom is sunny and cozy and looks out into the backyard. All Muriel gets is a view of the street. Still, she was the one who had first choice.

When I reached Rita's house I rang the bell. She opened the door and I said, "Hi, Rita. It looks like we're going to be sleeping on the floor again."

"What are you talking about, Sheila?"

"Where can we discuss that's private?"

"Outside," she said and grabbed a sweater from the closet.

We sat on the front steps and I told her how Bubbie is older than ever now, and can't take care of herself, and has to come and live with us and stay in my room.

"Oh, you poor thing," said Rita. "She'll be doing just what my grandmother does. She'll run around the house screaming at everybody — like a witch — and butting in all the time. Now you'll have two mothers trying to run your life. Just you wait and see."

"My grandmother isn't like that," I said. "She's really very nice. And I would love having her with us except that I don't know how I feel about giving up half of my room, and I *will* miss Myron and the Eskimo Pies."

"Well, Sheila. I guess nothing ever stays the same."

"That's for sure," I said. "Boy, it's going to be a long, cold winter."

Two

Bubbie moved in at the end of November. She came with her chair, a few plants, and a bagful of old photographs. That was all. Except of course for her clothes and her shoes. Everything else was either sold or given away because there was no room for them anymore.

As soon as the car pulled up in front of the house Muriel and I ran outside to give Bubbie a big welcome. Daddy took care of the suitcases and the plants and the chair while Mother helped Bubbie out of the car. Bubbie was holding her bag of pictures very close to her, almost hugging it. But she reached out to me with one arm when I came running up to her.

"Bubbie, Bubbie," I shouted, feeling glad to see her in spite of myself.

"Sheila dear," she said and drew me close.

7

"Why don't we all go in and get comfortable," Mother suggested.

Muriel picked up a suitcase and planted a polite peck on Bubbie's cheek. "Come on, Bubbie. I'll show you to your room."

Daddy brought in all of Bubbie's things and set the stuff down in the middle of the room, and Mother rushed about, showing Bubbie where to put everything. Then Bubbie said, "Well, my little Sheila, it looks like you've got yourself a boarder."

"Sheila's happy to have you with her, aren't you, Sheila?" Mother said.

"Of course, Bubbie. Of course I am."

"Okay, everybody, let's scoot," Daddy said. "Let's give Bubbie a few minutes to get settled before dinner."

"I'll stay and help her unpack," I said, anxious to see what was inside the suitcases.

"Oh, I don't know, Sheila," Mother said. "Bubbie might like to be alone right now. I don't think you should bother her."

"Sheila is never a bother," said Bubbie. "I would love her to stay with me."

"Well, all right. If you're sure she won't tire you out."

"Once she starts talking it's sometimes hard to stop her," Daddy added.

"It's good to have someone to talk to," Bubbie said.

"And good to have someone help me unpack my suitcases."

"I'll be in my room writing," said Muriel. "If you need anything, Bubbie, just call."

Funny how things can change and become completely opposite. Before, it was always Bubbie who was looking after me. On Saturdays when I came to visit, she would say, "Now what can I get you to drink? A glass of milk maybe? Are you sure you wouldn't like to take a little nap after such a long walk? Why not go up and see if Myron's home?"

But today it was as if Bubbie and I had traded places. She was the one who was coming here — to live. And I would have to help look after her. So now when the two of us were alone in the room I felt that I should say something. Only I didn't know what.

"Which suitcase do you want to open first, Bubbie?"

She didn't answer me. She just stood there looking around the room and then at her chair, clutching her bag of pictures so tightly, it seemed as if she'd never let it go. "Almost eighty years . . . and this is what's left," she said, and shook her head.

There was such a terrible sadness in her eyes that I found myself asking, "Which bed would you like to have, Bubbie? You can take your pick. Any one at all. Which one do you want Bubbie? Bubbie . . ."

"Oh, Sheila dear. I'm sorry. Were you talking to me?"

"Yes, Bubbie. I was asking you which bed you'd like to have. The one by the door or the one by the window?"

She sighed. "Oh, it doesn't matter to me. Any bed will do."

"But it doesn't matter to me either," I lied. "Go ahead and pick one." And as soon as I said that, I was sorry. What if she picked my bed — the one by the window? There are two windows on the wall. And my bed is under one of them. And it's just the right height for me to look out of when I sit up on my knees. How I love to wake up in the morning and be able to look right out of the window to see what the day looks like. To be right there to catch a snowflake or collect rainwater in a cup. To watch the sparrows build their nest under the window air conditioner across the way.

Bubbie looked at both beds and then she said, "Well, maybe the one by the window — if you're sure you don't care."

I swallowed. "I'm sure," I said.

Bubbie gently placed the bag of pictures on my bed ... I mean *her* bed, and then she turned to look at me. "Now, Sheila dear, remember, if you ever change your mind about the beds, you be sure to tell me. After all, this is your room."

"It's your room too, Bubbie."

Bubbie nodded slightly and looked around the bedroom. Then almost to herself she said, "Yes, my room too." Then she walked over to her chair and stood there, stroking it. I wanted to ask her about the chair; why she picked this particular one to bring here. I couldn't see what was so special about it. In fact, I thought it was a rather ugly old thing with enormously thick wooden arms and sides. And the red corduroy was rubbed off and worn-looking. I never liked it much. She had other chairs in her apartment. Nicer ones. Why this one, I wanted to ask. But I didn't.

"Where do you think we should put the chair?" I asked.

"How about over there," she said, pointing to the other window near the corner of the room. "Then I can sit and look outside whenever I have time."

"That sounds like a good idea," I said, and we dragged the chair over to the window.

Then we started on the suitcases. I was disappointed to find that she just had a lot of ordinary clothes in them — underwear and lots of flowered house dresses — which I guess is what I really expected to find, so I don't know why I was so disappointed.

Bubbie got half of everything I owned. Besides half of the room, she got half of my dresser, half of my bureau, and half of the closet. And if my drawers were a mess before the big changeover, you should've seen them afterward. Everything was all crowded and bunched together. And instead of having two junk drawers I was left with only one. The closet wasn't too bad. I take up very little room. Just a few blouses hanging here and there, and not many dresses. One or two maybe. Mostly I wear jeans, and I can put two or three pairs on one hanger.

Bubbie arranged her plants on the window sills. She had four of them and they were all the same kind. Purple Passion. The leaves are purple and they feel just like velvet. Bubbie loves Purple Passion, and she had them all around her apartment. I used to love going from plant to plant, pretending to be sewing the purple velvet on each leaf.

"Where are your other plants?" I asked. "You had lots more."

"I left them for the new people," she said. "So it shouldn't be lonely and empty when they move in. People shouldn't have to move into an empty place."

"I'm glad you brought some here, Bubbie. They liven up the windows."

Bubbie admired her Purple Passions. "Yes, they do look pretty. They even make a room look more like a home." Then all at once her face brightened and she said, "I have an idea. If you'd like I can show you how to make a cutting sometime."

"A cutting? What's that?"

"You cut a piece of the plant off, and from that one piece comes a whole new plant. You can grow your very own Purple Passion if you want to."

"Complete with velvet?"

"Complete with velvet. You won't even have to sew any on."

Then Bubbie laughed a little and hugged me, and I was only a little embarrassed that she knew about the sewing.

By the time we finished putting everything away it was dinnertime. And just as we were getting ready to leave the room, I pointed to my pictures of Famous Composers.

"I hope you don't mind my decor, Bubbie. I can always take them down if you want me to."

"Oh, don't do that," she said. "They've given the world such beautiful music." She walked over to my picture of Bach and stood there looking at him.

"Did you know," she said, "that Bach was so poor that one time, in Hamburg, Germany, when he was very young, he had to eat some herring heads that someone threw onto an old dirt road?"

"Herring heads?" I said. "Oh, the poor guy."

"You sometimes play one of his minuets, don't you?" Bubbie asked.

"Yes, Bubbie. Minuet Number Three." Then Bubbie started humming the minuet, and I hummed along with her, loving her for knowing so much about Bach. And pretty soon we were both humming our way into the kitchen.

Mother was tossing the salad and sampling it as she went along.

"Ah, the supper smells delicious," Bubbie said to her. "Let me help you with something."

"Thank you, Ma, but everything is done. You just sit down and relax and enjoy the meal."

The kitchen table is barely large enough to seat four people, and now that Bubbie was with us we had to start having our meals in the dining room. Which meant I had to be much more careful about eating. If I missed my mouth I might hit carpeting instead of vinyl.

We were all at the table ready to eat — that is, except for Muriel.

"I'm starved," I said. "When do we eat?"

"As soon as Muriel gets here," Mother said. "We all go our own separate ways during the day. The least we can do is have our dinners together."

"I'll get her," Bubbie said, getting up from her chair.

"No, Ma. It's not necessary. She'll be right along."

"You bet she'll be right along," I said. "She hasn't missed a meal in fifteen years."

Exactly two seconds later Muriel came running in. "Hi, everybody. Sorry I'm late. But I was listening to the news. And then, of course, I had to do a little writing."

"And how is my creative genius?" Daddy asked.

Muriel blushed. "Oh, Daddy."

Some creative genius. Daddy is an accountant. And even his columns of figures are more creative than Muriel's journal.

Everyboy ate and talked and acted very kindly toward Bubbie. Every time she got up to do something, Mother said, "Sit, Ma. I'll go."

Daddy said, "Is there something I can do for you, Ma?"

Muriel said, "Tell me what you want, Bubbie. I'll get it."

I wondered what would happen if Bubbie had to get up to go to the bathroom.

The second the meal was over, Muriel got right up to clear the table. Muriel has a thing about that. The food is hardly in her stomach and she's up and ready to do the dishes. Me, I like to sit back and relax and think about what I've eaten.

"Sheila, go help Muriel with the dishes," Mother said.

"Later. Just because she's ready doesn't mean I am."

"By the time later comes she'll be finished."

"Why can't she wait until I'm ready once in a while?"

"Because you're so pokey," Muriel said.

Bubbie got up from her chair. "Let Sheila and Muriel take a vacation today. I'll do the dishes."

"No, Ma. It's the girls' responsibility. Today Muriel washes and Sheila dries."

"I heard someplace that it's more sanitary to let the dishes drain," I said.

"That may be, but I don't like a cluttered counter.

Come on now, and go help Muriel."

"I'd be happy to do the dishes," Bubbie said. "I didn't do anything all day."

"I'll help her," Muriel said, as she shot me one of her uppity looks. "I for one am not afraid of a little work."

"Well, all right," Mother gave in. "But I don't want you girls shirking your responsibilities. And, Ma, I don't want you standing on your feet too long. Remember your veins. Sheila, you can make good use of the extra time by practicing piano. Your Hanon needs a little extra work."

"Okay," I said, and got out fast — before she had a chance to change her mind about the dishes. On the way to the piano I slipped into Muriel's room to get a peek at the latest entries in her private journal — hidden in its secret hiding place under her pillow.

9:00 a.m.	Bubbie's moving in today. Mother says to make her feel welcome. I'll carry her suitcase — if she has one.
12:20 p.m.	Elaine just called. She's going out with Jeffrey. Big deal. He's shorter than she is and has pits in his face.
3:30 p.m.	The room is getting stuffy. I'd better get out.
4:30 p.m.	Bubbie just came. I carried her suitcase. Sheila didn't carry anything. Bubbie's staying in Sheila's room. Not

	in mine, thank heavens. I need my privacy.
6:15 p.m.	I just finished listening to the news. I'm getting a headache. I wonder if I need glasses. Maybe I'm just hungry. I think I'll eat now and write more later.

Then from the dining room: "Sheila, I don't hear you practicing."

"I'm practicing, I'm practicing," I called as I ran out of the room and pounced on the piano. I closed my eyes and played some real dreamy music — of my own composition. It was heavenly.

"Sheila, that doesn't sound like Hanon."

"It is. It is. Listen. See, it's Hanon."

When bedtime came I undressed in the bathroom so Bubbie could have some privacy. When I got back to my room she was in her flannel nightgown, turning the covers down on my bed, her back toward me.

"Thank you for unmaking my bed, Bubbie."

She turned around and looked at me. Something had happened to her mouth! It was pushed together. It was like pudding. She smiled. "You're welcome, Sheila dear." Her words sounded funny, and I could see her gums. It was then that I noticed her teeth on the window sill. In a glass. I couldn't stand to look at them.

"Can I turn the light off, Bubbie?"

"Yes," she said. "Turn it off. I'm very, very, tired."

In the dark I said, "You know, Bubbie, I don't think Mother changed the sheets on your bed. She didn't expect you to be sleeping there."

"That's all right, Sheila. Sleeping on your sheets is like sleeping on my own."

"Gee, thanks, Bubbie. Even Muriel wouldn't sleep on my sheets."

"Good night, Sheila dear. Sleep well."

"You sleep well too, Bubbie." Poor old Bubbie. Poor old gums.

Three

Poor old me. I hardly got any sleep that night. The bed felt strange and Bubbie snored. So instead of jumping out of bed in the morning the way I usually do, I sort of dragged myself out after I heard Muriel's alarm go off.

For a moment I forgot where I was. It was only when I tried to look out of my window and it wasn't there that I remembered about Bubbie. She was still asleep in the bed that used to be mine.

I walked over to the other window to see what the day looked like, when I saw her teeth again. At first I thought of putting the glass behind the curtain or one of the Purple Passions, but I was afraid to touch it. And besides, Bubbie would wake up and not see her teeth and think she'd lost them.

19

I went to the bathroom, and when I got back Bubbie was up and the beds were made. A little while later she had her teeth in and her clothes on. She wore a fresh flowered dress, her heavy black shoes, and thick elastic stockings to cover up her varicose veins.

"Come, Sheila," Bubbie said. "I'll fix you some breakfast. I make good scrambled eggs."

"I know you do, Bubbie." Lots of times she made me scrambled eggs when I came to visit.

"That's because I use milk," she went on. "Milk makes them come out soft and fluffy."

"Can I have jelly on top of mine?"

"Jelly, ketchup. Anything you want."

"I'll take jelly."

"We'll ask Muriel if she wants eggs. I'll make breakfast for her too."

"You don't have to ask her, Bubbie. She'll eat anything."

While I was waiting for my eggs, I could hear Daddy gargling in the bathroom. He takes his sweet time every morning. That's because he's his own boss and can go to work whenever he feels like it. But when the tax season starts in January he's always working and I hardly ever see him.

My eggs were ready and Muriel walked into the kitchen just as I was drowning them in grape jelly.

"Good morning, Bubbie. Sheila, what on earth are you doing?"

"Putting jelly on my eggs."

"You're smothering them."

"No I'm not. I'm drowning them."

"What would you like for breakfast?" Bubbie asked Muriel.

"I'll have the same. I have to eat and run."

"Run where?" I asked.

"I have to talk to Elaine before school starts."

"Talk to her about what?"

"None of your business."

Muriel has this one friend. Elaine. Elaine is gorgeous! And she's fun to be with and has lots of friends — especially boys.

Now Muriel, well, she isn't fun to be with and she certainly isn't gorgeous. But she isn't ugly either. In fact, when people describe her they say she has a pretty face. Of course they leave out all the rest of her — which is to say she's a bit fat. I think her main problem, though, is her lack of imagination. She's a dud. I can't see what Elaine sees in her.

Pretty soon Mother popped into the kitchen with a bright and cheery "Good morning, everybody. Ma, you could have slept a little longer. I would have made breakfast for the girls."

Bubbie cracked Muriel's eggs into the bowl and began beating them. "You know how I love the mornings, Marion. I try not to waste them by sleeping late."

"Did you have a good night?" Mother asked her.

"I slept all right," Bubbie said, and she stopped beating the eggs. "But when I woke up it was so strange. At first I thought I was home. And then I remembered...."

Mother walked over to her and put her hand on her shoulder. "You *are* home, Ma. Just give yourself time." She reached for the bowl and frying pan. "Here, why don't you let me finish that and you can go sit down."

"No," Bubbie said, and her voice picked up again. "I promised Muriel some eggs."

Mother gave a little shrug. "All right. I'll go put up the coffee and we can have some breakfast."

For breakfast I knew just what Bubbie would eat. She'd have a kaiser roll and a cup of coffee. And I could just picture her hunched over the table, dunking the roll in her coffee and getting it all soggy before she nibbled on it. Easy for her teeth, I decided.

Muriel gulped down her eggs and ran out of the house. I almost yelled out, "I hope Elaine had a nice time with Jeffrey." A little while later Rita came to get me and I ran out too.

"So how's it going?" Rita asked. "With your grandmother, I mean."

"Everything's fine," I said. "Except for one thing. She's got the bed near the window."

"Aha! What did I tell you? I knew it."

"But it's not what you think. I said she could have it. It was my own idea. And you should see how nice she is to me. She even made my bed and fixed my breakfast this morning. And she knows all about Bach and she's going to show me how to make a Purple Passion cutting."

"Oh, sure," said Rita. "She'll be very nice to you — in the beginning. But just you wait. After a while you'll get on each other's nerves and she'll get picky and start hollering at you."

Boy, that Rita. She never lets up.

"Anyway," Rita went on, "at least you're saving your grandmother from the Old People's Home."

"The Old People's Home?"

"Sure. My mother told me about it when my grandmother moved in — against my wishes. She said that's where old people have to go when there's no other place for them to live. Or if they get senile."

"What's senile?" I asked.

"That's when you get old and your mind starts to go and you can't be reasoned with. Sort of crazy-like, but not really."

I wanted to ask Rita if her grandmother was senile, but it's not the sort of thing you go around asking people. So instead I just said, "How about sleeping over Saturday night? My folks are going out. We can go over to Forty Fantastic Flavors for some ice cream and read Muriel's private journal."

"Sounds great. Even though it's back to the floor again."

When I got home from school I found Bubbie giving the piano keys a bath. "I'm getting the keys nice and clean for you," she said. I watched her old wrinkled hand dip a sponge in a bowl filled with white liquid.

"What's that white stuff you're using?"

"Milk," she said, squeezing the sponge and making her knuckles look like little pointy mountains. "Nothing cleans piano keys like milk."

Bubbie was humming "The Anniversary Waltz" and running the sponge across the keyboard. "I have to hurry and finish before your mama comes home. If she sees me she'll worry that the sponge is too heavy to hold."

"Where *is* Mother?"

"She left with her dolls and said you should practice your piano."

"Oh, yeah. I forgot. Today is Mother's Doll Lady day." My mother is a B'nai B'rith Doll Lady. She has these dolls that look like famous people. And she goes around to all kinds of groups, like the Brownies and P.T.A. telling how these people helped the world and what they did for brotherhood. Mother is very big on brotherhood. Some of her favorite dolls are Jackie Robinson, Johnny Appleseed, and Golda Meir.

When Bubbie was finished with the keys, I sat down to practice. I started to do my Hanon. I really did. But somehow the notes that came out did not sound like Hanon at all. And they were beautiful. Then I heard something that sounded like a wrong note. It was Muriel's voice.

"Sheila, either quit fooling around and start practicing or let me have my turn."

"I'm not fooling around. I'm composing. Don't be such a grouch."

"Honestly! I can't understand why they continue to give you lessons. Two years and you still can't play anything."

"Look who's talking. Six years and all you know is 'The Happy Farmer.'"

"For your information, it's called 'The Joyous Peasant.'"

"It still sounds like 'The Happy Farmer' to me. Now go away and let me compose."

"You," she said, placing her hands on her hips, "are no composer."

"And you," I said, placing my hands on my hips, "are no writer."

She stared at me for a second. "And how would you happen to know that?"

"I... I guessed." Then partly because I wanted to change the subject and partly because I really wanted to know, I asked, "Muriel, how come I never see you happy? How come I never see you smile anymore?"

And she said, "What's there to smile about?"

★ ★ ★

That evening while we were doing the dishes, Muriel and I started arguing again. She was waiting for me to give her something to dry.

"A spoon, a fork, anything. Please."

I filled up a glass with suds and pretended it was a vanilla ice cream soda.

"Sheila, you're so pokey you're getting on my nerves."

"I'm in no hurry," I told her.

"Mother, *do* something," Muriel hollered.

"Okay, Sheila," Mother said. "Let's get moving."

"But it's not fair," I said, topping my soda with whipped cream. "Why should we do the same amount of dishes when she eats so much more than I do?"

"Mother!" Muriel sounded exasperated.

"Sheila, did you hear me?" Mother sounded annoyed.

Bubbie finished clearing the table and hurried over to the sink. "Girls, why don't you take a vacation today? I'll finish up for you."

"Another vacation? Gee, thanks, Bubbie."

"Ma, they don't need another vacation," Mother said. "And you don't need to be on your feet all day. Remember your veins."

"You won't let me forget them," Bubbie said, and shook her head. "I don't understand it, Marion. Everyone has veins. Why is it that you only worry about mine?"

"I can't help it, Ma. I care about you. I only want what's best for you."

"I know you're trying to be a good daughter, Marion. I only wish you wouldn't try so hard."

"I'll help Bubbie with the dishes and *we'll* be finished in no time," Muriel said, and shot me another one of her looks.

I guess Bubbie was really in the mood to do washing, because after she finished with the dishes she went to the bathroom to wash out one of her flowered dresses. But Mother caught her in the act and said, "You don't have to do that, Ma. We have an automatic washer."

"I know you do," Bubbie said. "But this is just one dress. I can wash it out and hang it over the tub and it will be nice and dry by tomorrow."

"That's nonsense," Mother said.

Bubbie went right on washing. "So it's nonsense."

Mother watched her for a while and then she said, "Here, let me have that. I'll put it in the automatic washer and in the automatic dryer, and it'll be easier for everyone." And with that, she pulled Bubbie's soggy dress out of the sink. Bubbie stood up straight, dried her hands, and without saying a word walked out of the bathroom.

For a long time I heard Bubbie in the bedroom, her slow, heavy footsteps going back and forth, back and forth. And then there was no sound at all. I tiptoed into the room. It was dark and still. Then from out of the darkness a quiet voice said, "Is that you, Sheila?"

"Yes, Bubbie, it's me. Did I wake you?"

"No, no. I haven't been sleeping. You can turn on the light if you want to."

Bubbie blinked at the sudden brightness. She was sitting in her chair and I could see that she had been crying. I wondered whether to leave or to stay. Sometimes it's hard to tell if a person wants to be alone or needs someone to talk to.

I wanted to say something to her, but I couldn't find the words. For a while neither of us said anything.

"You like that chair very much, don't you, Bubbie?"

"The chair?" Her eyes brightened and a smile appeared. "Ah, yes, Sheila dear. This chair is very special to me." She stroked the sides. "It doesn't look like much anymore. But it was very beautiful once."

"Is it very old?"

"Almost sixty years. It was the first piece of furniture your Zayde and I ever bought. Even before we were married. We saw it in a little shop and we bought it for ourselves for a wedding present. For a long time it was the only chair in the whole house and your Zayde and I took turns sitting on it."

Bubbie laughed as she told the story. It was as if she were making it happen all over again.

"I wish I could've known Zayde," I said.

"Oh, Sheila, you would have liked him so much. He was such a good man, always laughing and happy.

Come, I'll show you some pictures. He was such a handsome boy."

It was strange to hear Bubbie speak of him as a boy. But I guess she never knew him as an old man.

Zayde died a long time ago. I don't know too much about him, but I do know that he was born in Russia, and lived in a village not too far from where Bubbie lived. Only they didn't know each other then. He came to America, to New Jersey, when he was very young. So did Bubbie. And that's where they met and got married. Zayde died soon after Mother was born, so she never even knew him.

Bubbie took the bag of pictures out of a dresser drawer. "Many times I've meant to get an album," she said. "But I kept putting it off for tomorrow. And soon all the tomorrows turned into years. And see, the pictures are still in a paper bag."

She took the pictures over to her bed and spilled them out. Then we sat down to look at them. I had seen these pictures many times before, but I never got tired of looking at them.

There were pictures of Bubbie and Zayde as bride and groom, when Zayde really was a boy, and long before Bubbie started to worry and turn old-looking. There were family pictures of Mother as a baby, surrounded by her six older brothers. Some of the pictures were large and looked like they had been taken by a photographer. But most of them were ordinary snapshots of Mother and the boys standing in a park or on a front porch, stiff and smiley-looking.

There were so many pictures, and I wanted to look at them all. But it was getting late and there was one more thing to do before bedtime. Muriel was practicing piano—which meant that she'd be sitting there for exactly thirty minutes. No more, no less. And thirty minutes were more than enough.

I took my pajamas, and on the way to the bathroom I sneaked into Muriel's room to do a little light reading.

8:15 a.m.　I have to ask Elaine about her date with Jeffrey. Not that I really care.

3:30 p.m.　Elaine is in love with Jeffrey. She told me first thing this morning. I asked her to stay over Saturday night. But Jeffrey might ask her out. If he does she won't. But if he doesn't she will. I don't care what she does.

4:00 p.m.　Sheila's piano playing is getting me nervous.

6:30 p.m.　Sheila's giving me trouble with the dishes again.

7:30 p.m.　I should practice piano. I don't feel like practicing. I don't feel like doing anything. I feel empty. Why do I feel so empty? I think I'll go to sleep.

8:00 p.m.   I can't sleep. I think I'll eat something
            and try to practice. Maybe then I'll be
            able to sleep. I feel so alone. Why do I
            feel so alone?

I couldn't figure that one out. Why would Muriel
feel alone? She has me, doesn't she?

Four

Rita was right when she said I'd be having two mothers running my life. But she was wrong about my second mother. It wasn't Bubbie. It was Muriel.

Muriel didn't used to be such a bossy grouch. She used to smile a lot, and laugh. And there were times when she even seemed to like me a little. Then right around the time we moved to this house she started changing. She sort of crawled right inside herself and got quiet and touchy about everything.

Whenever I asked Mother what was wrong with Muriel she said it had something to do with the pains and anxieties of adolescence — whatever that meant. "In short," she said, "Muriel is growing up."

I got to worrying that maybe I would suffer the same pains and anxieties of adolescence while I was growing up, but Mother told me not to worry. I would turn out just fine. She said that growing up affects people differently and that even Muriel would turn out okay. She was just going through a phase and would grow right out of it. I only wished she'd hurry and grow out of whatever it was she had to grow out of. I couldn't stand her this way much longer.

I got to thinking about what Muriel wrote in her journal, about how alone she felt. And I got to thinking that maybe I could help her by letting her know that she wasn't really alone. That she still had me. But how could I tell her without letting her know that I read her journal? I'd have to think about that. And what would I do in the meantime? She was being impossible. Nothing I did was good enough. She said I spent too much time with Rita, and too much time daydreaming. But worst of all, I was lazy and selfish because I let Bubbie do the dishes for me and make my bed and dust the furniture in my room.

"Bubbie hasn't even been here a week yet and you've already made her your own personal slave," Muriel said to me on Friday after school. She was standing in the doorway of my room watching me change into my comfortable after-school jeans. Mother was out doing volunteer work at a hospital and Bubbie was in the kitchen baking my favorite Oatmeal Surprise cookies. Bubbie makes them for me pretty often because it's the only way she can get me to eat oatmeal. And her surprise ingredients, chocolate chips or raisins,

33

always make the cookies more interesting. Anyway, the part about the cookies is what set Muriel off.

"I have not made her a slave. That's an awful thing for you to say. Bubbie asked if we'd like some cookies and all I did was say yes. What's wrong with that?"

"You know that Mother doesn't like to see Bubbie standing for long periods of time. Especially in front of a hot oven."

"Well, Mother isn't seeing her. She's not home."

"There you go again. Just thinking of yourself. And it's not just the cookies I'm talking about. It's everything. It worked out pretty convenient for you, didn't it? Having Bubbie share your room and do your work for you. And Mother and Daddy saying what a good soul you are for giving up your privacy and not complaining. So noble and unselfish. It's disgusting."

I ran to the door and closed it. "Shut up, Muriel. She'll hear you. I never planned it that way and you know it. I like having Bubbie with me. And I *never* ask her to do things for me. She does them because she wants to. It makes her happy. She'd do things for you too, if you'd let her."

"I for one am not going to take advantage of her," Muriel said.

"Sure you will, Muriel. Later on you will."

"And what exactly do you mean by that?"

"You'll see. Later you'll be stuffing your mouth with those cookies, same as me."

"Oh, honestly," she said and stormed out of the room.

The whole house was filling up with the warm, rich smell of Bubbie's cookies, and I followed the smell straight to the kitchen. I could have found my way with my eyes closed.

Bubbie was standing at the stove, dropping spoonfuls of her Surprise cookie mixture onto a cookie sheet and humming. Her face was spotted with flour and so were her hands and arms. A couple of times I saw her wipe away strands of hair from her face and add another spot.

"Can I help you?" I called from the doorway.

"Of course," Bubbie sang out. "Why don't you see what else you can find to mix in here. All I have are raisins, so it's not such a surprise."

I rummaged through the cabinets and dug up some almonds and coconut shreds. "This is all I could come up with," I said, showing Bubbie what I discovered.

"Good," she said. "I'll drop in a little of each and you can mix everything together. We'll bake a lot of cookies so you'll have some for Rita when she comes over tomorrow."

"You know, Bubbie," I said while I was mixing, "the more junk you dump in, the better the cookies taste. You should enter your recipe in the Pillsbury Bake-Off."

Bubbie laughed and shook her head. "I'm afraid I can't do that," she said.

"Why not? Is it a well-guarded family secret or something?"

Bubbie laughed again, a little harder this time. "No, no secret. But you see, Sheila dear, I don't use a recipe."

"No recipe? Then how do you know how much of what to put in?"

Bubbie shrugged. "I don't know how I know. I just know. I use a handful of this and a pinch of that and a taste of something else. And it all comes out fine." Then she smiled gently and said, "I suppose when you've been cooking and baking for as many years as I have, you don't need a recipe."

When it comes to eating, Muriel has a fantastic sense of timing. As soon as the first batch of cookies was ready, she made her entrance.

"Muriel, honey, you're just in time," Bubbie said. "As soon as the cookies cool off a little you can have some."

Muriel looked from me to the cookies. Then she looked back at me. "Some other time, Bubbie. I think I'll have something else right now." And she headed for the refrigerator.

"You might like some carrots and celery," Bubbie said. "I cut some up for you and put them in a glass on the top shelf."

Muriel helped herself to a hunk of celery and stuffed it with peanut butter. She took a bite out of it and went back to her room.

For each batch of cookies to come out of the oven there was another batch to go in. Every time I looked at Bubbie she was bending over the oven door sliding a cookie sheet in or sliding one out. Her hair was damp with sweat and her face was flushed. But she was humming and singing and seemed to be having the most wonderful time.

I heard the back door open and Mother call up the steps, "Hello, I'm home."

Then I heard Bubbie say, under her breath, "Uh-oh, she's early."

"What a delicious smell," Mother said as she opened the kitchen door. "I could smell those cookies baking all the way outside." She took one look at Bubbie with her sweaty hair and red face and cried out, "Oh, Ma, you've been overdoing it. Just look at you."

"Don't worry, Marion. I don't plan on entering a beauty contest. Maybe just the Pillsbury Bake-Off." Bubbie winked at me.

"Ma, it's not funny," Mother said, looking around at all the cookies. "You've baked enough for an army. You must be exhausted."

"I feel fine. Sheila was a big help."

"I'm glad to hear that," Mother said, taking my hand and leading me to the sink. "Then she'll be a big help to me when she cleans everything up."

"Let Sheila take a vacation," Bubbie said. "I'll..."

"Oh, no. Not this time. I want you to lie down and take a little nap."

Bubbie looked at me helplessly. "You see, Sheila dear. First the mamas tell the children when to take their naps. Then the children tell the mamas when to take them. That's how it goes." And off she went.

I spent all of Saturday waiting for Rita to come over. In the morning I asked Muriel, "Can Rita and I sleep in your room?"

"Where does that leave me?"

"Well, you can have your choice. You can either sleep on the couch in the living room or you can sleep in my bed. I'll even change the sheets."

"No, thank you. I like my sleeping arrangements just the way they are. And don't go asking Bubbie to give up her bed."

"I wouldn't do that," I said. "Rita and I were planning to sleep on the floor anyway."

Rita came over just a few minutes before Mother and Daddy left. Mother gave us her last-minute instructions. "Don't give Bubbie any trouble. Don't give Muriel any trouble. Don't stay up late." And, "Have fun, kids."

"Can Rita and I go to Forty Fantastic?" I asked.

"All right," Mother said. "But go early. As soon as we leave, in fact."

"And make sure Muriel goes with you," Daddy added.

Muriel loves to go to Forty Fantastic, so I knew right away that she'd jump at the chance to come with us.

"No!" Muriel growled. "I don't feel like going with you. A couple of kids! I'll just stay here with Bubbie and you can bring us back something."

"You have to come with us," I told her. "Daddy said so. Rita and I are too young to be walking around by ourselves in the dark. If we end up getting kidnapped it'll be all your fault."

"Oh, all right. I'll walk with you, but I'm not going in."

Bubbie was watching TV—which was one of the few things Mother let her do without giving her an argument first. "We're going for ice cream," I said. "What can we bring back for you?"

"Something without nuts," she said.

"I guess nuts are hard on the teeth," I explained to Rita as we walked out the door.

Forty Fantastic is just two short blocks away from my house, and you'd think that just because I live so close I'd be in there all the time. But I hadn't gone since summer. You can get tired of anything, no matter how good it is.

"Let's get Lala Palooza Licorice," I said to Rita on the way over.

"It gets your teeth all black. How about Mustard Custard?"

"I had that one already," I told her. "And I never get the same flavor more than once. I plan on trying every flavor in the store. I have about nine more to go —if they don't bring in any new ones."

Muriel said she'd wait outside while Rita and I went in.

"What flavor should we get you?" I asked. I didn't have to ask.

"Vanilla," she said. "Two scoops."

While Rita was trying to decide between Mustard Custard and George Washington Cherry, I got one vanilla and one Lala Palooza, and I bought Bubbie a container of Blueberry Blintz.

Muriel and Bubbie ate their ice cream in the living room with the TV, and Rita and I finished ours up in my room.

"When do we get to read the journal?" Rita asked, taking a lick of George Washington.

"Later on. When Muriel goes into the kitchen to eat. She'll stay there for ages. Muriel's been eating a lot lately. More than usual."

"What's bothering her?"

"What makes you think something's bothering her?" I asked.

"Listen, Sheila, it's a well-known fact that some people overeat when they're upset or nervous. My mother, for instance."

"Could be," I said. "Maybe it has something to do with Elaine and Jeffrey and not sleeping over."

"Jeffrey was supposed to sleep over?"

"No. Elaine was."

After a while Muriel came into the room and told us to get out because Bubbie might want to go to sleep.

"And do something about your mouth, Sheila. Your teeth are all black."

Muriel went to her room and we heard the door close.

"Good. She's writing," I said. "That'll give us more to read."

Then very silently, Bubbie appeared in the doorway.

"Oh, hi, Bubbie. We were just leaving." I started to get off the bed.

"No, don't go," Bubbie said. "Stay here. Both of you." She walked over to her bed and pulled the sheets off.

"What are you doing?" I asked.

She carried the sheets out of the room and came back with fresh ones.

"What are all those for?"

Without answering me, she made up the bed and said, "There, all clean." And she turned around to leave.

"Where are you going, Bubbie?"

"I'm sleeping on the davenport tonight. You girls can have the room."

"Oh, no, Bubbie. Please. You can't do that. Mother will... I mean... Well, you shouldn't. Rita and I were planning to sleep on the floor. We always do. It's lots of fun. Really it is. Please, Bubbie...."

"Don't worry about it," Bubbie said. "The davenport is good for a change. If I had my way I would sleep on it all the time. It's nice and hard. Good for my back. You girls laugh and talk and have a good time."

"Your grandmother is nice," Rita said. "Mine is a witch."

For a while it looked as if Muriel was never going to get out of her room and we'd never get to read her journal. "I hate to disappoint you, Rita," I said. "But it looks like Muriel isn't as hungry as I thought."

I hardly got those words out of my mouth when I heard the refrigerator door opening and closing.

"Now?" Rita asked.

I nodded. "Now."

Rita and I took turns reading aloud. Softly, of course.

9:00 a.m. Sheila and Rita can't sleep in my room to-night and that's final. Elaine isn't sleeping over. Who cares? She's going out with Jef-frey — to a party. So what? Parties are so juvenile.

6:00 p.m. Sheila is getting ready for Rita. I bet Elaine is getting ready for Jeffrey. Who am I getting ready for?

7:00 p.m. I'm going to Forty Fantastic. But I won't go inside. Not with two little kids on a Saturday night. What if somebody sees me?

7:30 p.m. I just finished two scoops of vanilla. I don't even remember how it tasted. I think I'll do some reading.

8:00 p.m. Why are there sheets on the couch? Bubbie? That Sheila!

8:30 p.m. Elaine is at her party. Where am I? I am nowhere. I think I'll go eat something. Why am I always hungry?

"Look," I whispered. "She wrote about you three times. Twice by name."

"She's got you in there *four* times," Rita said.

I smiled. "I'm one of her most important characters."

We spent the rest of the evening laughing and fooling around, and Muriel kept banging on the wall, telling us to shut our mouths. Then Bubbie came in and gave us each a Surprise cookie and a cup of hot chocolate.

"Enjoy," she said. "And sleep well."

"Your grandmother really is nice," Rita said, and took a sip of the chocolate. "It was sweet of her to give up her bed."

"She's always doing things like that," I said. I took a sip of chocolate too and bit into my Surprise cookie. Not such a surprise, I thought, and pictured Mother walking into the living room. The big surprise is yet to come.

Five

Bubbie understands me. Sunday morning at breakfast she took the head of the smoked fish off before she gave it to me. Mother just slops the whole fish down on a plate. Head and all. And if there's one thing I can't stand it's a smoked fish with its head on and its eyes open. So I always yell, "Somebody get that fish's head off. He's staring at me."

Muriel, of course, always says, "Oh, Sheila, stop being so silly."

And Daddy says, "So what if he sees you? You don't look so bad in the morning."

But this time Bubbie took the head off and the skin too. She did the same to Rita's fish.

Mother hardly spoke to me at all during breakfast. She gave me one of her silent treatments. It wasn't hard to guess why.

"Sheila, I don't understand you," Mother said, after Rita left. "How could you give Rita Bubbie's bed and let Bubbie sleep on the couch?"

"But I didn't...."

"And another thing," Mother interrupted, "Bubbie is not our maid. From now on I want you to do your share of the dishes, your own dusting, and make your own bed. I want you to try to be more considerate — like Muriel."

"Like Muriel?" I screamed. "You think Muriel is so considerate. You think she's such a goody-goody, don't you? Just because she's fifteen and writes." And with that, I tore out of the kitchen and ran to my room to cry in private. I slammed the door, but then opened it a drop when I heard Mother and Bubbie arguing.

"Why did you yell at the child like that?" I heard Bubbie say. "I tell you over and over — I wanted to sleep on the davenport."

"There was no reason for you to give up your bed," Mother said. "It's a lot easier for little girls to sleep on the floor than it is for you to sleep on a hard couch."

Now Bubbie was doing something I never heard her do before. She was shouting at Mother. "Marion, I told you already, a hard davenport is good for my back. You just don't want to listen."

Next I heard the slow, heavy footsteps coming toward my room. I shut the door and sat down on Bubbie's chair to wait. I picked up a Purple Passion and ran my finger along the velvety leaves. There was a knock.

"Come in, Bubbie."

Bubbie opened the door and poked her head through the doorway. "Sewing another leaf?" she asked. I nodded and tried to smile.

Bubbie sat down on her bed next to me. "Not everybody understands us, eh, Sheila?"

"Nobody understands anything around here," I said. "Except when it comes to Muriel. Just because she's the oldest and she reads a lot and writes all the time. They even say she'll become a writer. And, Bubbie, she'll never become a writer. You should see the things she writes.... I mean... the things she probably writes.... I mean..."

"I know what you mean," Bubbie said, smiling.

"You do?"

She nodded.

"You won't tell, will you?" And as soon as I asked that, I was sorry. Of course Bubbie wouldn't tell. She's not that kind of person.

"Of course I won't tell," Bubbie said, as if she read my mind. "What a question."

"A stupid question. I know you wouldn't say anything. Do you think I'm awful? For reading Muriel's journal, I mean."

"No, not awful. Maybe just a little curious. That's all."

"I don't even know why I bother to read her journal.

46

She doesn't write anything good."

"Maybe she has nothing good to write about," Bubbie said. "Maybe when good things start happening to her, her writing will change. Maybe she'll change. Who knows?"

"Boy, I can't wait until I get to be fifteen. Maybe Mother and Daddy will start listening to me once in a while." And then it hit me. "Oh, no! When I'm fifteen she'll be twenty. See, I'll never catch up to her."

"Oh, you'll catch up all right," Bubbie said. "Someday it will all even out. Just you wait and see."

"How can you be sure, Bubbie? How are you able to know so many things?"

"I know from experience, Sheila dear. With age comes experience. A lot of experience and a little wisdom." She gave my knee a little pat. "Now," she said, and got up from the bed, "you wait here and I'll be back in a little while. We'll do something to cheer you up."

I sat back in Bubbie's chair and stroked the velvety leaves of the Purple Passion. Then I set the plant down on my lap and ran my fingers along the edges of Bubbie's chair, along arms that were too thick, along corduroy that was old and worn. Bubbie's chair. Zayde's chair. It wasn't such an ugly old chair after all.

In a few minutes Bubbie came back with a small knife and a small jelly jar partly filled with water. As soon as she took the Purple Passion from my lap I knew just what we were going to do.

"We're making a cutting, aren't we, Bubbie?"

"That's right," Bubbie said, examining the plant. "Come help me pick out a nice, healthy stem. With lots of leaves."

I found a stem with six very velvety leaves. "How's this one?" I asked, showing Bubbie the one I picked out.

"That's a good choice," Bubbie said. "Here now. Take the knife and just snip the stem off the plant."

I took the knife and stood there holding it. "I don't think I can do it, Bubbie. It's like cutting off someone's arm." I shuddered at the thought.

Bubbie let out a little laugh. "You won't hurt the plant. In fact, you'll help it grow even better. Go ahead now. Just snip off the stem."

"Well, okay. If you say so." I cut the stem off the plant and Bubbie told me to put it in the jar of water, making sure not to get the leaves wet.

"In a few weeks your Purple Passion will have roots, and you'll be able to plant it in a pot," Bubbie told me.

"Are you sure it'll work?" I asked, putting the jar on my dresser.

"Sure I'm sure. Where do you suppose *my* plants came from?"

"I thought you bought them."

"I bought some of them, but most came from cuttings, just like yours. When you grow the plants from cuttings you don't have to buy so many."

I couldn't get over how many things I was finding out from Bubbie. And about Bubbie. She makes new plants from old ones, she doesn't use recipes, she knows about composers, and she shouts. How lucky for me she didn't go away to an Old People's Home.

A week later, just after breakfast on a mild December day, Bubbie put on her coat and announced that she wanted to visit her old neighbors in the apartment building.

"We'll drive you," Mother said. "Sidney and I are going downtown and we can drop you off."

"Sure, Ma," Daddy said. "We'll be glad to do it. We go right by there anyway."

Bubbie waved them off. "Thank you, but no. It's such a beautiful day, I feel like taking a nice, long walk."

"That's just it," Mother said. "It *is* a long walk. Back and forth — it's too much for you. We'll drive you."

"If she takes it easy it can't hurt her," Daddy said to Mother.

"Sidney, it's twelve full blocks. If she feels like walking she can go around the block a couple of times. But it's nonsense for her to walk twelve blocks when she can ride."

"Thank God I still have the use of my legs," Bubbie said. "I'll walk and I'll be fine."

"I tell you, that's nonsense," Mother said.

"You're right," Bubbie said. "It *is* nonsense to walk so far. I changed my mind anyway. I'll stay home."

"We'll drive you," Mother insisted.

"Some other time," Bubbie said, and she sat down.

Before Mother and Daddy left, Mother tried again. "Are you sure you don't want to come with us?"

"Thank you. I'm sure," she said.

As soon as Mother and Daddy were out the door, Bubbie got up and grabbed her coat. "So — I changed my mind again," she said before I had a chance to ask. She opened the kitchen door, and just before she started down the steps she turned around and winked at me. "I'll tell Myron you said hello."

When I came home from school Mother and Bubbie were in the kitchen arguing. Bubbie must have just come home because she still had her coat on.

"It would have been so easy for us to drive you," Mother was saying. "But no, you had to walk back and forth, all alone. Something could have happened to you. What then?"

"Nothing happened," Bubbie said, unbuttoning her coat. "I'm old, but I'm not helpless. I wish you would stop treating me like an invalid."

"And I wish you wouldn't be so stubborn."

"I'm almost eighty years old," Bubbie answered her. "I've earned the right to be stubborn." And she walked out of the kitchen.

One cold morning a few days later, I was searching

for a pair of tights to wear under my jeans. I had to dump out an entire drawer before I finally found one pair without holes in the toes. I was just getting ready to throw the rest of them away when Bubbie said, "If you give them to me I'll sew up the holes for you."

"Thanks, Bubbie. Because after today this pair won't be any good either. I keep forgetting to cut my toenails."

While Mother was making breakfast, Bubbie was sitting at the kitchen table sewing up my tights.

"Why don't you sit by the window?" Mother suggested. "The light is better."

"I can see fine right here," Bubbie said.

Mother tsk-tsked a little, but went on to finish breakfast. By the time I was through eating, she was tsk-tsking even more. "Ma, that's enough sewing already. You don't need to do any more. You'll strain your eyes."

"Marion, leave me alone already. Please."

"But they're not worth the trouble. They were cheap tights."

"You're right," Bubbie said, getting up from the chair. "You're always right. So there's no use arguing with you. I'm too tired to argue with you anymore." She dumped the tights in the garbage and went to her room.

Then, partly because of what she said to Bubbie, and partly because I didn't like the idea of her buying me cheap tights, I gave Mother a tsk-tsk and went off to school.

The first snow of the season fell that day. It fell white and heavy, and I could hardly keep from looking at it and wondering if it was good packing snow.

To pass the time, Rita and I slipped notes to each other during class.

Look out the window. Do you see what I see?
Sheela

You are invited to a snowball fight. My house. After school.

Reeta

Can't. I've got something else in mind.
Sheela

After school I ran home, sloshing through the snow in my sneakers. Luckily I had my mittens. They were still in my pockets from last year. I gave the snow a packing test by making a snowball. Perfect. Then I ran into the house looking for Bubbie and getting snowy footprints all over the vinyl and carpeting.

"Bubbie, Bubbie," I shouted. "Where are you?"

"In here, Sheila dear."

I ran into the bedroom and found her sitting in her chair. She looked so alone sitting there by herself.

"Bubbie, put on your coat and your boots. We're going to make a snowman."

"A snowman?"

"Yes. Right out in the yard in front of the window. Just you and me."

"How wonderful," Bubbie said. "I haven't done that in years. And when we come in I'll make us some hot soup."

I waited for her to put on her winter things and we went out into the yard. I didn't bother with boots because my feet were all wet anyway.

Bubbie started on the snowman's head while I was working on his middle and bottom. While we were rolling the snowballs I asked, "Where's Mother? Is she being a Doll Lady again?"

"No," said Bubbie. "Today she left with her pictures."

Not only is Mother a Doll Lady, she's also a Picture Lady. She goes around to schools with copies of famous paintings and talks to kids about the artists.

The snowman's bottom and middle were finished. And just as Bubbie was lifting up the head, there came a loud rapping at the window. Mother and Muriel were in my room, looking out. They were pounding away like mad. I thought for sure they'd break the window. I smiled and waved. They didn't wave back. Then just as the snowman's head went on they both came running out into the yard.

"Ma, Ma," Mother was shouting. "Stop! That's enough. Are you looking for trouble?" She grabbed Bubbie by the arm and led her to the house. "What do you think you were doing just now?"

"I know what I was doing. I was helping Sheila with her snowman. And such a nice snowman it would have been if only you stayed away a little longer."

All the way back to the house Muriel kept saying, "Oh, Sheila, how could you?"

While Bubbie was taking her things off in the hallway, I went into the kitchen to take off my sopping sneakers. Underneath the sopping sneakers were sopping tights with toes poking through the holes. I sat down on the floor and warmed my feet by the heating vent. While I was wiggling my toes, Mother asked, "Whose idea was it to build a snowman?"

"Mine," I said. "I thought it would be fun for Bubbie."

"But, Sheila, surely you know better than that. How could you let an eighty-year-old woman build a snowman?"

"She's only seventy-nine," I said. "And it's a very small snowman."

Mother put up a pot of water to boil. "Sheila, honey, do try to understand. Bubbie is getting on in years. She shouldn't overdo. And she will if we don't watch her. That's the whole purpose of having her come to live with us. So that we can keep an eye on her. She doesn't know her limitations. Old people are some-times like that. They think they can do the same things they did when they were younger. And they can't."

"But she was sitting in her chair with nothing to do," I said. "And she seemed so lonely. She hardly ever has anything to do."

"I'm afraid that building a snowman isn't the answer."

"Maybe I could teach her how to play the piano."

"That's just plain silly," Muriel said. "She's too old to learn a musical instrument."

"Not only that, but she's got arthritis in her fingers," Mother added. She poured the hot water into a glass, added honey, lemon, and a tea bag, and took it to Bubbie.

When Muriel and I were alone in the kitchen she acted the part of second mother again. "Sheila, I wish you'd stop making trouble. Stop making waves."

"What kind of waves am I making?"

"You know what I mean. You're causing all kinds of problems, the way you act with Bubbie. This business with the snowman, for example."

"I'm not causing any problems, Muriel. The problems are already here. Bubbie likes to be busy and she doesn't have enough to do. I'm just trying to help her out a little. And it's more than you're doing. All you do is hide out in your room all the time. You don't even care about what's going on in the rest of the world."

"That's not so," she said angrily. "I do too care. Even in this country there's hunger and poverty and unemployment and natural disasters. I care plenty about the world."

"That's not the world I'm talking about," I said, and went to my room to see Bubbie. She was sitting in her chair looking out at the snowman.

"Such a nice snowman," she said. "Too bad he has no face."

"I'll go out in a while and give him one, Bubbie."

"What will you use for eyes?"

"Do we have any black olives?" I asked.

"Black olives? Yes, I think we do."

"Then we'll use black olives."

Bubbie looked at me and laughed. "Expensive eyes," she said.

There were two things I learned during the next few days.

1. Sugared water is better for a cough than hot milk.
2. If you snore while you sleep on your back, sleep on your side and you might not.

Here's how I came to find these things out. By the time the snowman had a face on his head I had a cold in mine. Then it traveled to my chest. Muriel said I got sick from my wet sneakers. But I said there was a lot of something going around in school and I must have caught it.

One night I dreamed I was at the beach swimming in the ocean. I was coughing and coughing and I couldn't stop. I kept drinking the ocean water, but it was salty and it made me cough even more. And all these thousands of people kept looking at me and moving away because I was so contagious. And pretty soon I was the only one left in the whole ocean, and I was still coughing and coughing and drinking and drinking....

"Drink this, Sheila. Wake up and drink this."

"It's too salty. It makes me cough."

"It's not salty. It's sweet. Drink it, Sheila, and you'll feel better."

It was Mother. She's always there with hot milk whenever I get one of my coughing spells. So I drank, and the coughing stopped. But what was I drinking? It didn't taste like milk. A cool hand touched my forehead and cheeks. The voice came through clearer now. "There, that's better, isn't it?" Then I knew that the voice and the hand were Bubbie's. And instead of hot milk there was sugared water. Bubbie came with her sugared water the next couple of nights too. And each time she stopped my coughing and put me to sleep.

In the beginning I was too sick to do anything but sleep. Even when Daddy came in each morning to ask, "What can I bring you after work today?" I told him that I didn't want anything. But as I got better, the days dragged by. I watched my Purple Passion grow roots and tried to keep busy with Muriel's journal. Some parts I even read twice.

8:00 a.m.	That Sheila! Imagine. Expensive black olives on a snowman. I could have eaten them.
4:30 p.m.	That Elaine! Practically ignored me all day. She's with Jeffrey every minute.
5:00 p.m.	Sheila is really sick. Lucky her. No school. Telephone — for me. I'll be back. I'm back. It was Elaine. Talk, talk, talk. All about Jeffrey. She doesn't stop.
8:00 p.m.	Telephone — for me again. Elaine is going out with Jeffrey. New Year's Eve. I am going nowhere.

But mostly the days were empty and dull with nothing to do. And it was awful having nothing to do, having to sit around the house all day. Just like Bubbie. The days were empty for her too. She took lots of naps and I watched her sleep. I noticed that she only snored when she slept on her back. Whenever she turned on her side she stopped. I don't like to see Bubbie sleep on her back. It's not just because of the snoring. That doesn't bother me too much anymore. But seeing her on her back frightens me. It reminds me of being dead. A couple of times Bubbie was on her back and she wasn't snoring, so I thought she died. I kept staring at her chest, watching for it to go up and down as proof that she was still alive and breathing. I wish she'd sleep on her side all the time and not scare me like that anymore.

Besides sleeping, she sat in her chair and looked out at the snowman with the olive eyes. Together we looked at her pictures, and that's when she seemed happiest. So the next time Daddy asked, "What can I bring you today?" I had an answer.

"I've been thinking about it, Daddy, and I know just what I want."

"Okay, name it and it's yours."

"A photo album," I said.

Six

The album was red with gold trim and had room for refills. Bubbie smiled when she saw it. "It's beautiful," she said.

"Daddy bought it for you," I told her.

He also bought a package of gold photo corners that would look terrific against the black pages. I was glad he didn't buy the kind of album with plastic pages. Bubbie would be finished filling them with pictures in no time. But in this album she'd first have to put corners on the pictures and then paste them in. And the corners would dry up and fall off, just the way they did in my scrapbook, and Bubbie would have to start all over again. A project like that could keep her busy for a long time — maybe even a year.

It was nice to see Bubbie having such a good time licking the corners, pasting in the pictures, and humming "The Anniversary Waltz." I guess she was a very fast licker and paster, because it took her a little less than a year to stick in all the pictures. It took about four days. But we spent all of winter vacation looking through the album, starting from the very beginning.

There were lots of pictures of Mother growing up in New Jersey, on the chicken farm in Lakewood. There was one of her when she was about seven or eight years old and she was carrying a suitcase.

"Where was she going?" I asked Bubbie.

"No place. She was coming back."

"From where?"

"From running away from home."

"Why was she running away from home?"

"I don't even remember now. But she packed a suitcase because she was running away and was never coming back."

"But she came back, didn't she? I mean, she's here now."

"Oh, yes. After an hour she crawled out from under the porch and said she was hungry."

"Sounds like something Muriel would say."

Bubbie turned the pages and continued with her stories. "That picture was taken the day before your mother fell rear first into a pail of hot water. I do believe she would still have her scar. And that was taken the day after she fell down the stairs and knocked her front teeth out."

"You mean all those things happened to *Mother*?" I asked, wondering if Mother knew about her scar.

"Oh, yes. Those things and many more too. But I can't remember anything else just now."

Together Bubbie and I watched Mother grow up and get married. We saw Muriel and me as babies, and my aunts and uncles and cousins who are still living on their chicken farms. For me it was like reading a book that Bubbie had written.

"How come you moved away from Lakewood?" I asked.

"When your mother got married and left, we missed each other very much. And she asked me to come here to live."

"Didn't you miss the farm?"

"Oh, yes. And I missed the rest of my family. But they all had each other. And mothers feel a special closeness to their daughters, you know. So I left everything and came to this city."

"I'm glad you did, Bubbie."

"I'm glad too. It was good being close to you and Muriel, and watching you grow up. It was very good."

Was good. Bubbie said it *was* good. Did that mean it wasn't good anymore?

We finished looking through the album by the second week of January. Now what was Bubbie going to do for the rest of the year?

Mother was no help. She still wouldn't let Bubbie do much around the house. Once when she had to go away she asked Bubbie to put the roast in the oven at three o'clock. And another time she said she was expecting a phone call and would Bubbie please take the message. And when the painters came over, would she watch to make sure they didn't take anything. But that was about all.

Once in a while if the weather wasn't too bad, Bubbie and I would go out for a walk. It was always best to go out when Mother wasn't around so she couldn't nag us about staying out too long or walking too far.

I loved taking walks with Bubbie. Because that's when she told stories about herself when she was a little girl in Russia. And if it was hard to imagine Mother as a little girl, it was next to impossible to imagine Bubbie as one.

Once Bubbie told me about the time there was a parade in her village.

"It was the first parade I ever saw in my life," she said. "Oh, the music, the people. It was wonderful. So I followed the parade, and followed it. And the next thing I knew I found myself in an orchard. All alone in an apple orchard. I don't even know how I got there."

"Weren't you awfully scared, Bubbie?" I asked.

"Oh, I was so frightened. I remember there were

gates. So many gates. And I kept going in and out of gates, until finally I recognized some houses in the village and was able to find my way home. And let me tell you, Sheila, I never followed another parade after that."

Then Bubbie laughed and seemed to feel better for the whole day.

But some stories didn't make Bubbie laugh. One time she told about the pogroms, the terrible attacks on her village. She told how angry mobs would come into the village where the Jews lived, and burn and rob and kill people. And everyone would have to hide. "One time," said Bubbie, "we hid in the cellar behind the sacks of potatoes. We could hear the angry people above us shouting and breaking things. But we couldn't do anything. We couldn't whisper or sneeze or even breathe too loudly. They would have killed us. The mothers, the babies, everyone. Many people were not as lucky as we were."

After I heard that story I imagined Muriel and me hiding in our basement behind sacks of potatoes, trying hard not to breathe.

On one of our walks Bubbie bought me a clay pot and a package of potting soil. Roots had already sprouted on my Purple Passion. It was a healthy little plant and Bubbie said it was ready for potting. When we got home Bubbie helped me pour in the soil and plant the Purple Passion. "Give it plenty of sun and be careful not to water it too much," she told me.

I set the plant on the window sill next to hers. I thought about how nice it was to have a Purple Passion of my own and not have to worry about rubbing all the velvet off.

But mostly Bubbie just sat around the house. She sat in her chair and looked out of the window. There wasn't much to look at. Our snowman was all melted and his olive eyes were gone. I asked Muriel if she ate them but she just snarled at me.

Sometimes Bubbie sat in front of the TV, but her face was blank and I could tell that she was looking but not watching. She sat very close to the set, and I worried a lot about radiation. But Rita told me, "It takes about fifteen or twenty years for the radiation to build up. And your grandmother is seventy-nine already so there's not much chance of her getting any."

I didn't like to hear Rita talking that way. I didn't want to think that there might ever come a time when Bubbie wouldn't be around.

And Bubbie, my Bubbie who loved the mornings, began waking up later and going to sleep earlier. And she took longer naps during the day. Every night before she went to sleep I could hear her muttering something to herself. But I couldn't make out the words. They didn't seem to make sense. Something was happening to Bubbie. Was she getting senile? Is this what Rita was talking about? I kept watching for signs that she was senile, but I didn't know what to look for, exactly. She didn't act crazy or anything. Just sad.

Nobody else seemed to notice that anything was wrong. Daddy was getting busy with his taxes and was hardly ever home. Mother was busy with her dolls and her pictures. And she was doing a lot of marching.

Mother is a marcher. She goes around to all the houses in the neighborhood, collecting money for charity. She marches for Cancer and Cystic Fibrosis and all kinds of diseases. She feels it's the least she can do to show how grateful she is for a healthy family.

One day in February when Mother was getting ready to go out collecting for The March of Dimes, I asked, "Why don't you take Bubbie with you? She might like it."

"It would be hard for her to walk so much," Mother said. "Besides, I can cover the territory so much faster myself."

Muriel probably didn't notice anything because she either kept herself locked up in her room or was busy eating. Bubbie kept a constant supply of carrot and celery sticks around the house in strategic locations. In addition to the ones in the middle of the top shelf in the refrigerator, she had them in glasses on the counter and on the kitchen table. But Muriel rarely took the hint. She usually managed to work her way around the carrots and celery to find more appetizing and fattening foods.

One day after school she found me in the kitchen heating up a can of vegetarian vegetable soup.

"You're supposed to dilute that," she informed me, looking over my shoulder.

"I like it condensed," I told her. I took the pot and spoon over to the table and began eating. She sat across the table and watched me.

"Want some?"

"No. Watching you eat that makes me lose my appetite," she said as she reached for a carrot stick.

Nothing can make you lose *your* appetite, I said to myself. "You sure you don't want some soup, Muriel? For once in your life you ought to do something daring."

"Oh, this is ridiculous," she said, getting up from her chair. "Me sitting here with you talking about soup."

"Then let's talk about something else."

She sat down again. "Like what?"

"I don't know. There must be something we can talk about. We're sisters, aren't we? Sisters are supposed to talk to each other, aren't they? We *never* do. How come you never tell me things, Muriel?"

"Tell *you*? Sheila, you're ten years old. How can I confide in a ten-year-old? You wouldn't understand anything."

"Sure I would. I understand a lot. I know all about the pains and anxieties of adolescence."

"Where did you hear that?"

"Oh, just around. It's got something to do with growing up. And if you can explain things to me, maybe you can make it easier for me when my time comes."

"Explain things to you? I can't even explain anything to myself."

"Well, just tell me what it feels like to be an adolescent."

She put what was left of her carrot stick on the table and stopped chewing. "Happens? Nothing happens. That's just it. For me nothing's happening. I just sit here eating and getting fat. But don't worry. For you it'll all work out. Just like it does with Elaine. Things are always happening for her. She's got Jeffrey, and she's into everything. Cheerleading, baton twirling, everything."

"So big deal. What's so great about cheerleading and baton twirling. I think they're dumb. It's like somebody asking you what you want to be when you grow up and you say, 'My great ambition in life is to become a cheerleader and a baton twirler.' "

Muriel let out a little giggle. "Or how about someone asking what you majored in when you were in school, and you say, 'I have a degree in cheerleading and baton twirling.' " And we both burst out laughing.

"See how much fun it is to talk?" I said. "We should do it more often."

It really felt good to be talking with Muriel like that,

and I decided that I might never get a better chance to tell her something that might make her feel less alone.

"Muriel," I began, "I never told this to a single soul before, but sometimes I wake up in the middle of the night and get all scared thinking about what would happen if Mother and Daddy died, and how I'd miss them and how alone I'd be. And then I remember that I'd still have you and that we'd have each other, and neither of us would really be alone."

"Oh, Sheila. Do you really?"

"Well, not so much now. But when I was younger."

"Don't worry, honey. That won't happen."

"Sure. I know." It was the first time she ever called me honey. Maybe one day I really would catch up to her.

After that day of shared confidences, Muriel became touchy and irritable again, full of the pains and anxieties of her adolescence. And then one day she smiled at me. For no reason that I could think of she just came home from school and smiled.

"Hi, Sheila."

"Huh?"

"I said, hi, Sheila."

"Oh. Sure. Hi, Muriel. You okay?"

"Couldn't be better," she sang out. "Say, Sheila, you can ask Rita to sleep over Saturday night if you want. And you can have my room. I'll sleep in your bed. And you don't even have to change the sheets."

"Gee, thanks, Muriel. I'll ask her today."

Then, still smiling, she danced out of the kitchen to her room without so much as a glance at the refrigerator. Even through the closed door I could hear her singing.

Boy, she's losing her mind, I thought. That Muriel is really cracking up. And I ran over to ask Rita about sleeping over.

4:00 p.m.　Jeffrey has a friend. Ralph. Elaine wants to know if I'm interested. Maybe for Sat. night. That's tomorrow. I said sure, why not? Ralph — nice name. Elaine says he has a nice face.

8:00 p.m.　Phone call from Elaine. It's definite for Sat. night. That's tomorrow. A party. A party!! I don't think I'll be able to sleep tonight.

* * *

8:00 a.m.　Today's the day! I didn't sleep a wink. What should I do with my hair? I'll set it to look like I didn't set it.

10:00 a.m.　Too excited to eat breakfast. Can't decide what to wear. My old jeans are too tacky. My new jeans are too new. I hope I smell nice.

1:00 p.m.　What will I talk about tonight? Shall I be sophisticated and say hello Ralph, or be

cute and say hi Ralph? I'm not sophisticated. But I'm not cute either.

7:00 p.m.   I'm ready. I don't want to go. My hair
looks like I set it. My jeans are too tight.
Maybe I washed them too much. Ralph
will be here between 7 and 7:30. Maybe I
still have time to call Elaine and cancel.
There's the bell. Too late! Help!

"Well, that explains a lot of things," I whispered to
Rita Saturday night.

"Why are you whispering?" she asked. "Muriel's already left."

"Oh, yeah. I forgot. That explains a lot of things," I
said again. "That explains the extra-long shower, the
hot comb, and her brand-new jeans that she put
through six hot-water washes."

"And that explains her good mood yesterday," Rita
put in. "But how will she act toward you tomorrow if
she has a rotten time tonight?"

"I'm afraid to think about it," I said, putting the
journal back under the mattress where Muriel hid it
especially for the night.

We flopped down on Muriel's bed. "What does
Ralph look like?" Rita asked.

"I haven't the slightest idea. Muriel chased me away
when he rang the bell. She said she didn't want me
standing around gawking at him."

At about nine o'clock I went in to say good-night to

Bubbie. I opened the door just a crack to hear if she was sleeping. I didn't want to say good-night and wake her. I listened very carefully. There were no sounds of sleep — no heavy breathing or snoring. But one sound did come out of the room. It was the sound of Bubbie crying.

I didn't know what to do. I had never heard Bubbie cry before. I'd seen her tears, but I had never really heard her cry. I wanted to go to her, but I couldn't. She wouldn't want me to find her that way. So I closed the door and stood outside the bedroom.

I heard Mother and Daddy talking in the living room. I should tell them, I thought. They would know what to do. They could fix it so Bubbie wouldn't cry anymore. But maybe it wasn't right for me to tell them. Maybe it would be like telling a secret you were trusted with. Like breaking a promise. So I went into Muriel's room, turned off the light, and got into bed.

Rita's voice came out of the darkness. "Hey, Sheila. What's going on?"

"I'm tired," I said. "I'm going to sleep."

In the darkness Bubbie's crying came back to me. I shut my eyes, and way deep inside myself, I cried too.

We had a quiet breakfast the next morning. Daddy was in bed catching up on some sleep, Muriel didn't say much, and Bubbie didn't show.

Rita left as soon as she finished eating. About an hour later she called me.

"When can I come over?"

"You just left."

"I know. But I'm dying to get a look at Muriel's journal and find out what happened last night."

"If she writes anything interesting, I'll let you know," I said. Though for some reason, I didn't think I would.

Muriel kept to herself most of the morning. One time she sat down at the piano and played a few notes. But she never really played any music.

When she was finished, I asked, "How was your date with . . . what's his name?"

"Ralph," she said. "His name is Ralph. And it was nice, Sheila, really nice. We're going out again tonight. He's taking me to Forty Fantastic. Ralph absolutely loves Lala Palooza Licorice."

A couple of times Mother asked Muriel, "Did you have a good time, dear?"

And each time Muriel answered, "Oh, yes, Mother. I really did."

Mother didn't seem to be paying too much attention to Muriel's answer, though. She seemed to have her mind on something else. I wondered if she found out about Bubbie's crying.

"Sidney," she said when Daddy finally got up, "Ma hasn't eaten a thing all morning. This is the second breakfast she's missed this week."

"Well, maybe she's just not hungry today. I can't

think of any law that says a person can't skip breakfast once in a while."

"If you ask me, I don't think she's very happy," I said.

"Why would you say a thing like that?" Mother asked.

They didn't know about the crying. But maybe they should know. Maybe that's the only way they could help Bubbie.

"Last night...she was crying," I said.

"Sheila, why didn't you tell us before?" Mother asked.

"I didn't want to worry you."

"Well, now I really am worried."

"You know," Daddy said, "it just might be that what Ma needs is some elderly companionship. Some nice lady with whom she'd have something in common."

"You might have an idea there," Mother said. "There must be at least one other lady her age who lives close by."

Mother and Daddy were going to help Bubbie. I felt better already. I helped myself to some cream cheese that was on the table. "How about Rita's grand-mother?" I said with my mouth full.

"How about Sheila's former baby-sitter, Mrs. Nussbaum?" Daddy suggested.

"No, dear, I don't think so. From what I've heard, she's getting quite hard of hearing lately and refuses to wear a hearing aid. Ma will have trouble carrying on a conversation with her."

I poured myself a glass of milk to wash down the cream cheese. "Rita's grandmother," I said.

"How about that nice lady, Mrs. What's-her-name who used to be your dressmaker before her eyesight started to fail her?"

"Oh, you mean Mrs. Bloom. I'm not too sure about her either. She constantly complains about her aches and pains. And she often gives detailed descriptions of her examinations at the doctor."

"Rita's grandmother," I said again.

"How about that lady who runs the little fish store across the street from Forty Fantastic? She must get pretty lonely spending her days with a lot of smelly fish."

"She wouldn't be very cheerful company for Ma. All she talks about are people she knows who are either sick or who have passed away."

I got up from the table to leave, but decided to give them one more chance. "How about Rita's grand-mother?"

Mother looked up into my face. "What was that you said, Sheila?"

"I said, how about Rita's grandmother?"

"Rita's grandmother! Why, yes, of course. Mrs. Plumb. Now why didn't I think of her before? She's perfect."

"Except for one thing."

"What's that?"

"She's a witch."

"Now, Sheila, that's not a very nice thing to say about a person."

"It's not my opinion. That's what Rita says. I never stick around her long enough to find out if she's a witch or not."

"Well, witch or no witch, I'm going to get the two of them together one of these days."

Bubbie came out of her room to have lunch with Muriel and me. Mother was so glad to see her that right away she gave her a kaiser roll with a fresh cup of instant coffee. I watched her dunk the roll and chew on it. Nibble, nibble. Dunk and chew.

It was good to have her back.

When she was finished she sat back in her chair and looked at Muriel. "So, Muriel, you had a nice time last night. I can see that."

"Yes, I did, Bubbie. And we're going out again to-night. We're meeting at Forty Fantastic."

Bubbie was with us for dinner too. Muriel left the table early because of her date with Ralph. After a while I got into my pajamas and waited for her to come home.

When she got back she was smiling and her teeth were all black.

"Your teeth are all black," I told her.

"I know," she said, laughing. "You should see Ralph's."

Muriel walked me to my room. Bubbie was in her nightgown, turning down the covers on her bed and muttering to herself again. She was saying something in sort of a singsong way. This time she was still wearing her teeth, so I was able to make out the words.

"Eat and sleep, eat and sleep. Life is nothing but eat and sleep."

Seven

Bubbie cried again that night. I pulled the covers over my head but the crying still came through. I told Mother about it in the morning.

"That settles it," she said. "I'll call Mrs. Plumb today and invite her for lunch."

Mrs. Plumb arrived that very afternoon just as I was leaving for school. She came in through the front door as I slipped out the back door. She was still there when I got home. I heard her talking as I walked in through the back door and up the steps.

"...vacationing in Bermuda, she was, poor thing. Need I tell you what a sight it was to see her lying in the box like that, so cold and still, with that beautiful suntan of hers...."

When I walked into the kitchen I saw them both sitting at the table. In front of Bubbie was a glass of hot tea. Mrs. Plumb had tea too, only hers was in a cup.

Bubbie was nodding and taking little sips of tea while Mrs. Plumb's thin mouth went on talking, talking, talking, never even taking time out to swallow. Her thin pasty face looked especially pasty. Maybe that was because her reddish hair looked especially reddish. She probably uses some cheap stuff to dye her hair because some of the coloring rubbed off on her collar.

When Bubbie finally noticed me, she waved me over and gave the seat next to her a few pats. Mrs. Plumb stopped talking about her dead friend and smiled her thin smile at me. I walked over to the chair and sat down next to Bubbie. Mrs. Plumb gave me a long, hard look.

"You don't wear dresses either, do you, dear?" she asked.

I looked down at my jeans to see what was wrong with them. She went right on talking to Bubbie without even waiting for me to give her an answer. "Well, no wonder," she went on. "Why should she be any different? All the girls are the same. My Rita lives in pants too. I don't believe she owns a single dress. In our day, if you remember, girls dressed like girls. Now they all run around in pants."

"Times have changed," said Bubbie.

"For the worse, if you ask me. How can you expect girls in pants to grow up and become great ladies like

Eleanor Roosevelt? You don't think for one moment that Eleanor Roosevelt wore pants, do you? Did you ever see a single picture of her wearing pants? Even when she rode horses she rode in dresses. Or skirts. But certainly not in pants."

"Her dresses didn't make her the person she was," said Bubbie. "Even if she wore pants, she still would have been a great lady."

"A great lady," Mrs. Plumb repeated. "That she was. Yes indeed. A great lady and a dear friend."

"Eleanor Roosevelt was your friend?" I asked, wondering how a great lady could be friends with Mrs. Plumb.

"She shook this very hand," said Mrs. Plumb, admiring her right hand. "We once met at an election rally and she spent almost the whole afternoon listening to my opinions of world affairs. I found we had a lot in common. I'm sure we would have become close friends had she lived longer."

When Mrs. Plumb finally got around to leaving, she told Bubbie to come visit with her soon and that they shouldn't be such strangers. Then Bubbie took two aspirins and went to bed, and I went into Muriel's room to read her journal. It wasn't much. It was full of Ralph.

Ralph	Ralph	Ralph	Ralph
Ralph	Ralph	Ralph	Ralph
Ralph	Ralph	Ralph	Ralph

Ralph and Muriel   Muriel and Ralph
Ralphie and Muriel   Muriel and Ralphie

When I got through reading, I could think of just one word. Yech!

Bubbie spent a lot of time in her room during the next few days, and one afternoon Mother finally convinced her to take a walk over to Mrs. Plumb's house to return her visit. "She's called several times asking for you," Mother said.

So Bubbie went to see Mrs. Plumb. And she went the next day too. And the next and the next. Almost every afternoon when I came home for lunch I'd find Bubbie wearing one of her best flowered house dresses, her hair nicely combed with a neat little bun sitting on the back of her head. She'd give her cheeks a little pinch to give them color, and then she'd put on her black coat and hum her way out the door.

"Mrs. Plumb has done wonders for Ma," I heard Mother telling Daddy one evening.

"Your grandmother has done wonders for my grandmother," I told Rita one morning on the way to school.

"What are you talking about, Sheila?"

"Your grandmother and mine," I said. "Ever since *my* grandmother has been going over to see *your* grandmother, she's been a different person. A happier person, anyway."

"But she hasn't," Rita said.

"Hasn't what?"

"Hasn't been coming over. In fact, *my* grandmother does nothing but complain that *your* grandmother said she wouldn't be such a stranger and promised to visit her soon. And it isn't even soon anymore and she still hasn't come."

"Not ever?"

"Not ever."

"Well, where does she go every afternoon? If she's not at *my* house and she's not at *your* house, where is she?"

The next day I gulped down my lunch and waited for Bubbie to pinch her cheeks. Then she put on her coat, said good-bye, and hurried out the door. I waited about half a minute and ran out after her.

Bubbie was walking down the street toward Rita's house. But when she reached the corner she turned left instead of right. At first I followed her from behind, but I was afraid she'd look over her shoulder and see me there, so I crossed the street and followed her from the other side. She walked steadily ahead and the wind blew and flapped her coat and she pulled the collar up around her neck. I tried to pull the collar up around my neck too, but I couldn't because I wasn't wearing any collar. I wasn't even wearing a jacket. I had forgotten to put one on because I was in such a rush to get out of the house.

When I reached the end of the next block I hid behind a lamppost that had a sign wrapped around it:
LITTERING IS FILTHY AND SELFISH SO DON'T DO IT. I
waited there and shivered and watched Bubbie as she
turned the corner and disappeared down the steps of
J. Morgan Antiques.

J. Morgan Antiques is tucked away in between a
dear little flower shop and a heavenly smelling bakery
where they make the most delicious charlotte russes.
It's a dark shop with a rusty metal awning over the
door and a window filled with all kinds of old things,
lamps and vases and statues.

Rita and I used to stop by every so often on the way
home from school, and we just loved to go inside and
look at the lovely old clocks and the china cats and
listen to the music boxes that Mr. Morgan sometimes
played for us.

Mr. Morgan was always happy to see us. And he
never minded our looking around as long as we didn't
touch anything or bring our charlotte russes into the
shop. He's a friendly sort of person. And quite old.
Sort of an antique himself, really, with a red blotchy
face under a pile of snow-white hair. He looks like a
strawberry shortcake.

I stood at the lamppost and waited for Bubbie to
come out of the shop. But she didn't. It was getting
late and I was still shivering, so I hurried back to
school.

I followed Bubbie the next few days too, and it was always the same. She went into the shop and never came out.

But then one day I didn't have to worry about getting back to school on time. It was Monday and we had the whole day off because of teachers' conferences. I arranged to meet Rita by the Littering Is Filthy and Selfish sign.

"I bet you think I'm a pretty awful person to be spying on my own grandmother like this," I said to Rita.

"Not at all. You're just looking after her. Let's cross over so we can get a *better* look."

We walked across the street. "I hope she's not doing any foolish buying," Rita continued. "It's hard to tell the difference between a genuine antique and a piece of junk."

We crept down the steps of J. Morgan Antiques and stood with our bodies against the brick wall and our heads poked around to where the door was. We took turns peering into the shop, but neither of us could see anything. Only our own reflections.

I was on my second look when suddenly the door opened and a head popped out. It was Mr. Morgan. "Looking for something, girls?"

"An antique!" Rita blurted out. "We came here to look for an antique. Didn't we, Sheila?"

"Oh, an antique," said Mr. Morgan. "And what kind of antique did you have in mind?"

"A gumball machine," I said quickly. "An antique gumball machine. From the olden days. Around the Fifties."

"That's right," said Rita. "Not a phony. Not a new one made to look old. But a genuine antique."

"Well, I don't know about a gumball machine," he said leading us into the shop. "But maybe I can interest you in a nice chocolate mousse."

"Chocolate moose?" I asked, tripping over the welcome mat and picturing a stuffed chocolate moose head hanging up on the wall.

"Yes, chocolate mousse," came a voice from the other end of the room. "Come and have some with us."

The voice was Bubbie's, and she was sitting at the counter and laughing. Mr. Morgan disappeared into a back room while Rita and I dragged two chairs over to the counter. Before we even had a chance to sit down, he reappeared with two small dishes and then suddenly began shouting at us. "No, no, no. Not the Chippendales!" He quickly set the dishes on the counter and began pushing the chairs away, almost knocking us over.

"Heavens, no. It wouldn't do to get chocolate mousse on my Chippendales, now would it? I'll get you something much better. "And he brought out two card-table chairs from the back room.

Rita started on her moose as soon as she sat down. I just stared at mine.

"Go ahead and try it," said Bubbie. "It's very good."

I took a taste of my moose. It was cool and creamy. Better than chocolate pudding.

"This *is* good," I said.

"It should be," said Bubbie. "Mr. Morgan is a gourmet cook."

"Come, come," said Mr. Morgan. "Look who's talking about being a gourmet. You should see your grandma here. She made us some stuffed cabbage the other day. The best I've ever tasted. And her apple strudel!" — he kissed his fingertips — "superb. We certainly have been having a delightful time exchanging recipes."

"Delightful, " Bubbie agreed. "Every day we have something different. Sometimes just a dessert and sometimes a whole meal. And always, always everything is delicious. You should see."

"You can see tomorrow," said Mr. Morgan. "I'm making a cheese souffle and you're all invited for lunch."

Rita and I got up to leave and Bubbie said she wanted to stay to help Mr. Morgan with the dishes.

On our way out, Mr. Morgan called to us, "I'll see if I can find one."

"Find what?" Rita and I asked at the same time.

"A gumball machine."

We giggled and ran out of the shop and up the steps. Then suddenly my giggles turned into laughter and I began shouting, "Oh, Rita, Rita, Rita, don't you feel just wonderful? Don't you feel all warm and good inside?"

"Yeah, I feel all right. The mousse was a little rich, though."

"Oh, Rita, Rita, Rita. Don't you see? Don't you understand? My grandma has a boyfriend."

Eight

"Do you think they'll get married?" I asked Rita on the way to J. Morgan Antiques the next day. I told my mother I was having lunch with Rita, and Rita told her mother she was having lunch with me. "Do you think my grandma and Mr. Morgan will get married?"

"I think you're jumping to conclusions, Sheila."

"But it's possible, isn't it? I mean, they might. Old people get married too, don't they?"

"Well, even if they'd want to get married, I doubt that they could afford to," she said. "I read somewhere that if two old people are getting money from social security and want to get married, they can't because the government would take the money away from one of them and they'd starve together."

"But that's not fair," I cried. "That's not the least bit fair."

"It's got nothing to do with fair. It's a government

88

law. Your grandmother would lose her social security and they'd have to live on Mr. Morgan's single meager check."

"My folks would never let my grandma and Mr. Morgan starve," I told her. "I'm sure they'd help them out. Especially during the tax season."

J. Morgan Antiques smelled delicious that afternoon. Better than the bakery. Bubbie was already there, unpacking a carton of figurines. When she saw us she smiled. "Hello, come in. You're just in time. I think Ju — Mr. Morgan is just about finished with the soufflé and we can eat soon."

"Good," I said. "I'm starved."

Bubbie went back to her unpacking, and Rita and I went over to look at the miniatures. Mr. Morgan has a glass case filled with the dearest little animals: elephants, cats, dogs, and birds — mostly birds — all painted in soft, quiet colors. And there are shelves of miniature rooms — bedrooms and dining rooms with tiny chairs and tables and even settings of cups and saucers on lace tablecloths. Oh, how lovely the rooms are. It takes your breath away just to look at them. Each one looks so real, you feel as if you could walk right in.

The miniatures have been there ever since I can remember. That's because they're not for sale. Mr. Morgan said that the whole collection belonged to his late wife, so of course he'd never think of selling any of it. And I'm glad. I think that's just about my favorite thing to look at in the whole shop. Rita's too.

Suddenly from the back room a voice sang out, "Ta da!" And there was Mr. Morgan standing with his cheese soufflé. Then Bubbie sang out, "Julius, it's beautiful. A masterpiece."

"Well, I'm a little out of practice," he said, carrying his masterpiece over to the counter. "But I have to admit it came out pretty good."

It didn't look like much of a masterpiece to me. It was a high, puffy sort of thing. Like nothing I'd ever seen before. I nudged Rita. "I wonder what a cheese soufflé tastes like."

"Me too. But I guess we'll have to eat it to find out."

At first we couldn't eat it because it was too hot. And then when I finally got a taste of it, I decided I didn't like it much. "I'd rather have a hot dog," I whispered to Rita.

"Hot dogs aren't gourmet," she whispered back.

The four of us sat there eating our soufflé, and Mr. Morgan was saying how he loved to do fancy cooking but ever since his wife died there was no one to cook fancy for. "You just don't bother to do fancy cooking for yourself, when you're all alone. The satisfaction comes from seeing other people enjoy your food."

Bubbie nodded in agreement and Mr. Morgan went on about how he sometimes cooks for his son and daughter-in-law when they come to visit, but it's really a waste because they don't appreciate fine cooking the way his wife did.

"Julius," Bubbie began, "do you remember, in the old country, the stoves people used to cook on?"

He took his glasses off and began polishing the lenses with a paper napkin. "Ah, how well I remember. Great big brick ovens standing up against the wall. We used them for cooking and baking and for keeping the house warm in the winter. And since I was the eldest, it was always my job to bring in the wood and light the fires to keep the oven going. Those winters were cold, let me tell you."

"Bitter cold," Bubbie said. "But the ovens were so warm. I remember when I was little how I used to sleep right on top of the oven. All of us children took turns sleeping there."

"That's fascinating," Rita said.

"But, Bubbie, how could you sleep on top of the oven? Didn't you get burned?"

"No, Sheila dear, the fire was at the bottom of the oven and all around it was brick. Even now I can remember how warm my bed on the oven felt to me."

Mr. Morgan put his glasses back on and he and Bubbie sat there, lost in their own thoughts.

Rita and I went to J. Morgan Antiques only twice after that. The first time Mr. Morgan made us spinach crêpes, filled the center of each one with a glob of creamed spinach, and folded the sides over.

When Bubbie saw them she said, "Look, Sheila, like blintzes."

They did look like blintzes. Except that they were

flatter and thinner, and blintzes are usually filled with sweetened cottage cheese. I never tasted them with spinach before, but they were delicious.

The second time we went there Mr. Morgan said we were in for a rare treat. Turtle. As soon as I heard "turtle" all I could remember was the smell of my turtle when it died. I couldn't eat a turtle. Rita and Bubbie couldn't eat one either. Mr. Morgan was the only one who could. "You really ought to try some," he kept saying. "You might never get another chance. Turtle is very hard to come by. Expensive too."

But the rest of us kept saying no thank you and settled for a tossed salad topped with chopped egg. Mr. Morgan said that chopped egg was the mark of a good salad.

After that day Rita and I didn't go back to J. Morgan Antiques anymore. Bubbie did, though. She went to see Mr. Morgan every afternoon except Sunday. It was funny the way Mother always said, "You and Mrs. Plumb have a nice time now." And Bubbie would smile at me, or wink, and I would laugh inside myself.

Mother told Bubbie that since she's been going to Mrs. Plumb's so much lately it would be nice to invite her to our house for a change. And Bubbie said, "Mrs. Plumb lives closer to the park."

It was fun sharing Bubbie's secret—for as long as it lasted. But I should have known it wouldn't last long.

Nine

"But I don't understand, Mrs. Plumb. She's with you, isn't she?"

"I wouldn't come looking for her if she were with me. I can assure you, I'm quite alone."

I had just opened the back door one afternoon a few weeks after Mr. Morgan tried to get us to eat turtle, and heard Mother talking with Mrs. Plumb. I sat down on a step and listened.

"But she left for your house not long ago," Mother went on. "She should be there by now. Isn't she usually at your house by this time?"

"By this time? She's not at my house at any time."

"But I don't understand. You've been seeing each other practically every day for weeks."

"My dear. The last time I saw your mother was that afternoon you invited me for lunch. I don't know who she's been seeing, but it certainly hasn't been me."

"But I thought. . . . Well, I guess I've misunderstood. Of course, that's it. There's been a misunderstanding. I'm sure there must be some explanation."

Mrs. Plumb, you have a big mouth, I said to myself. And I waited for her to walk out the front door so I could walk in through the kitchen door.

Mother didn't mention anything about Mrs. Plumb's visit until later that evening. We were all finishing dinner, except for Daddy who was working late. Mother brought Bubbie a glass of tea and told her not to sit in the draft.

"I'm not sitting in the draft. I'm fine."

"Then put a sweater on."

"I don't need a sweater."

"You'll get chilled."

"I won't."

"Mrs. Plumb was here this afternoon."

"Oh?"

"So?" Mother said to Bubbie.

"So?" Bubbie said to Mother.

"Dinner was great tonight," I said to both of them.

"Maybe we should talk in the living room," Mother suggested.

"We can talk here," said Bubbie. "There's nothing to hide from the girls."

"All right then, Ma. I'll get to the point. Where have you been all these afternoons?"

"Gee, it's too bad Daddy had to miss this great dinner we..."

"Sheila, shut up about the dinner already," Muriel shouted at me. "Mother asked Bubbie a question."

"And I'll answer the question," Bubbie said. "I've been with Mr. Morgan in his antique shop."

And Bubbie went on to tell about that very first day when she discovered J. Morgan Antiques and J. Morgan too.

"I was on my way to see Mrs. Plumb because you wanted me to. But I just could not bring myself to spend another afternoon with that woman. So I went the other way and walked around by myself and looked in the store windows. Then I came to that small antique shop in the basement. And, Sheila, I tell you, it was just like the shop where your Zayde and I bought our chair before we were married. It brought back such memories that I had to go inside.

"I saw a man — he turned out to be Julius — crawling around on the floor, and when he saw me he said, 'I'll be with you as soon as I find my glasses. A man owns one pair of glasses... you'd think he'd be able to keep track of them.'

"I noticed that he had a pair of glasses on his head, so I said, 'Maybe you're wearing them.'

"He felt around his head and said, 'Ah, so I am. I always forget them way up here. I guess it's a sign of old age.' He got up from the floor and said, 'Now... is there something I can help you with?'

"I told him that I came to his shop to look — not to buy. And he said if I wanted to look, then he'd be happy to show me around. And did he show me! Every piece in the shop. And with each piece there was a story to go with it. How he got this and who gave him that. There was too much to see in one day so I went back the next day and the next and the next. There was always so much to talk about. We talked about all the beautiful old things that he collected, and we talked about the old country. And then one day, just like that, he invited me to stay for lunch. I've been staying ever since."

"You should see," I said. "He has a stove and a refrigerator, and he makes chocolate mousse and turtle and..." Oops — I wasn't sure I should've said anything.

"What was that about chocolate mousse?" Mother asked.

"Yeah," said Muriel, crunching a carrot stick. "And what was that about a turtle?"

"Uh...well, Rita and I went into the shop one day and we met Bubbie there and had chocolate mousse, and one day there was turtle but I didn't have any."

"We've met there many times, haven't we?" said Bubbie.

"Why, you little..." Mother said to me and began laughing. "You knew about this all the time. Why didn't you say anything?"

"You never asked," I said. I admit it wasn't a very original answer, but she caught me by surprise and I didn't know what else to say.

"Well, I know the shop," Mother said. "It's been there for years. Strange, though, I've never gone inside. And I've never met Mr. Morgan."

"He's nice," I said. "And he's a gourmet cook. We've had soufflé and spinach crêpes and..."

"Does he run the shop by himself?" Mother asked.

"He used to, long ago," said Bubbie. "But now his son takes care of the business and Julius comes in a few hours every afternoon. Just to keep busy."

"But, Ma, I still don't understand. Why didn't you tell me all this before?"

"And if I told you? What then? Another argument. Don't go, it's too far, it's too much for you...."

"But, Ma, if he's a good friend of yours he should be a good friend of ours too. We'd like to meet him. Maybe we can invite him to dinner one day this week. How's Friday?"

"I wonder," said Muriel, "as long as you're inviting, do you think we can ask Ralph to dinner sometime too?"

"Okay," said Mother. "How's Thursday?"

"Thursday's fine," said Muriel.

"That settles it," said Mother. "Thursday Ralph, and Friday Mr. Morgan. This should be an interesting week."

Ten

Bubbie was full of smiles and hummed a lot around the house. Mother bought her a new pale-blue dress without a single flower on it.

Muriel was disgustingly agreeable to everything I said or did. There was this one time I sat down to practice piano and I found myself playing the most heavenly music I had ever composed. Mozart would have turned green with envy, it was so beautiful. I sat there with my eyes closed and played—on and on until I heard Muriel singing off key in the hallway. I quickly switched to Hanon.

Muriel came dancing into the room. And of all things, she said, "Oh, Sheila, don't stop. I love what you were playing just now. Please finish it."

"Gee, Muriel, I don't know if I can get back in the mood."

"Do try, Sheila, please."

So I tried, but it was no use. The notes just wouldn't come. "I think you broke the spell," I told her.

"Oh, I *am* sorry, Sheila."

"That's okay. Maybe it'll come back to me."

Muriel sat on the edge of the piano bench. "You know, Sheila, I never realized it before, but you really do compose some pretty good music. You might even become a composer someday."

"Maybe," I said. "Unless I decide to become a cheerleader or a baton twirler."

"You're a little nut," she said, and put her hands on my shoulders and gave me a squeeze. She was quiet for a couple of seconds and then she said, "Sheila, do you remember what you said that day? About my becoming a writer? Well, you were right. I'm no writer. I like to write in my journal, for myself, but writing isn't what I really want. And anyway, I don't think I'm creative enough."

"I bet you'd be good in politics, though. I don't think you have to be creative to be in politics."

"Oh, Sheila, do you really think so?" she said and slid over closer to me. "Because that's just what I've been thinking about. A career in politics. I think someday I might like to go to Washington and work for some representative or senator. Just for starters of course. And after that, who knows? I might even become a senator or representative myself."

"That's a terrific idea, Muriel. Can I have your room when you leave?"

"You *are* a nut," she said. Then she gave me a hug and left the room.

On Thursday we were all together for breakfast, even Daddy who overslept. Mother was planning the menu for Ralph.

"Let's see now," she was saying. "We'll have meat loaf, baked potatoes, tossed salad..."

"Don't forget the chopped egg," I said. "Mr. Morgan says it's the mark of a good salad."

"Very well then. A tossed salad with chopped egg, broccoli..."

"Mother, no," Muriel shrieked. "Not broccoli. Boys don't like broccoli. It's a feminine vegetable."

"Broccoli is feminine?" I asked. "How can you tell?"

"Sheila, don't be funny. You know what I mean."

"I'm a boy and I like broccoli," Daddy said.

"Daddy, please."

"All right," Mother said. "What do you suggest?"

Muriel thought for a while. "Peas and carrots."

"Okay," Mother said. "Dull but okay."

"Why don't we have both?" Bubbie suggested. "Broccoli for the girls and peas and carrots for the boys?"

"That's the best idea yet," Mother said. "We'll have both."

5:00 p.m.   Ralph will be here in exactly one hour. I can't wait to see him. I wonder what flavor lip gloss I should wear. Raspberry. Ralph likes raspberry.

* * *

I put the journal back under the pillow and turned to leave. The door opened before I got to it, and there in the doorway stood Muriel. Her lips were practically dripping from her raspberry lip gloss and she overdid her eyes too. It looked like she used Magic Marker for eyeliner. I especially noticed her eyes because she was using them for glaring at me.

"Exactly what were you doing here in my room?" she demanded.

"Nothing, Muriel. Just looking at the pictures on your wall. I see you've got a lot of new ones."

She stopped glaring and smiled at me with her drippy lips.

"Aren't they nice? I just love them. Bubbie cut them out for me. Wasn't that sweet of her?"

I shrugged and walked out of the bedroom. Mother was putting her finishing touches on the dining room table.

"Boy, it's getting to look more and more like Democratic Headquarters in there every day," I said, pointing to Muriel's room.

The doorbell rang and Muriel ran from her bedroom to answer it. I ran after her. Muriel opened the door and in walked Ralph holding a single red rose.

"For you," he said, handing Muriel the rose. Then he looked at me and smiled.

"Hi. You must be Sheila."

"Hi," I said. "I am." I tried hard not to look at him too much. I didn't want Muriel to think I was gawking at him. I tried hard not to notice that he was shorter than Muriel — and thinner. I tried hard not to notice that I liked his smile.

"Come on and say hello to the rest of the family," Muriel said, leading Ralph up the steps and into the living room.

Ralph went around the room shaking hands with Mother, Bubbie, and Daddy who took off work special. Muriel was standing off to the side, sniffing her rose.

"I guess he couldn't afford to buy you a whole dozen. Huh, Muriel?"

"Sheila," she said, and took another sniff. "When you get older you'll realize the significance of a single red rose. It's the romantic thing to do."

After a while Mother, Daddy, and Bubbie left the room and I was alone with Muriel and Ralph. "Don't you have somewhere to go or something to do?" Muriel asked me.

"No, nothing I can think of."

"Why don't you go help Mother with the dinner?"

"She doesn't need me. Bubbie can help her."

Muriel gave me a disgusted look and went over to the piano. I sat down next to Ralph, who smelled of soap and toothpaste, and watched him as he was picking the cashews out of the mixed nuts and listening to Muriel play "The Happy Farmer."

She played the song three times without stopping, so it would seem longer. By the end of the third time Bubbie came into the room and announced that dinner was ready.

The table looked lovely with the individual salads topped with chopped egg. Mother used her best dishes — the ones she usually saves for holidays and important company. And instead of a plastic tablecloth and paper napkins, she used her good linens.

Daddy must have really been hungry because he was the first to sit down. He spread the napkin on his lap and was all ready to dig into his salad. But Ralph gallantly walked over to Muriel and helped her with her chair. She seemed absolutely delighted. And then, of all things, he helped me with my chair too. Nobody ever did that for me before. I felt kind of special. I felt that I could really get to like Ralph.

As soon as Daddy saw what Ralph did, he got up and ran over to help Mother and Bubbie with *their* chairs. Daddy never did that for them before and they seemed surprised. But they sat down looking very pleased.

Ralph sat in between me and Muriel. We were eating our salads and for a while nobody was saying anything. All you could hear was the sound of lettuce being crunched. A few times I caught Ralph and Muriel holding hands underneath the table. And then Ralph leaned over to Muriel and I heard him say,

"Sorry about that single rose, Muriel, but I just couldn't afford a whole dozen." I almost choked on a crouton. I knew for sure I would get to like Ralph.

I think the reason people always invite each other to lunches and dinners is because if they run out of things to say they can always talk about the food. Four times Daddy said please pass the salt, and three times Mother asked each of us if we wanted French or Thousand Island with the salad. And Muriel, the same Muriel who couldn't care less what she shoved into her mouth, kept showering Mother with compliments. "Oh, Mother, everything here is just delicious. The meat loaf is just right. Not too well-done and not too rare." But the best part of the whole evening came when Muriel was passing the food to Ralph and she held the dish of peas and carrots out in front of him.

"Peas and carrots?" Muriel asked.

"No thanks," Ralph said. "I'll take the broccoli."

I liked Ralph.

Mother said that the whole evening went very well, and she seemed honored that Ralph had second helpings of everything.

By lunchtime on Friday Mother was frantic. She recleaned the house and began worrying about dinner and wondering if a roast was good enough for Mr. Morgan.

"Don't fuss so," Bubbie said. "The house looks fine and Julius will enjoy anything you make. He's just so happy to be invited."

But mother insisted on fussing, and when Bubbie offered to help she said no thank you and told her to rest up for the big evening ahead. I think Bubbie was in too good of a mood to argue with her.

"Believe me," she said when Bubbie went to lie down, "it's no easy task preparing dinner for a gourmet. I wonder how Mr. Morgan prefers his meat. Probably rare. Gourmets like rare meat. Or maybe it's medium-rare. I just don't know. Well, maybe it really doesn't matter that much anyway."

But it does matter, I said to myself. Everything matters. This whole evening matters. Everything has to be perfect for Bubbie. And I decided to go over to J. Morgan Antiques to find out how Mr. Morgan likes his meat.

Mr. Morgan said he would be with me as soon as he took care of the customer who was looking for a miniature painting suitable for framing. When the customer left without the painting, Mr. Morgan asked, "Now, Sheila, what can I do for you?"

I didn't feel like asking about the meat right away. You just can't go up to a person and say, "How do you like your meat?" So I said, "My grandma probably won't be in this afternoon. She's resting up for dinner."

"Well, that's a good idea," he said. "I'm looking forward to this evening with your family very much."

"So's my grandma. She even bought a new dress. It's pale blue and it's beautiful. The only thing wrong is that it's too plain. There's not a single flower on the whole dress. And my grandma does love flowers." I said that hoping that Mr. Morgan would bring Bubbie a single red rose, like Ralph brought Muriel.

Then I decided I'd better find out about the meat. So I said, "Mr. Morgan, can I ask you something? How do gourmets like their meat? Rare or medium-rare?"

He laughed a little and said, "I don't know if there's an answer to that. I guess it's all a matter of taste. But I happen to like mine medium-rare."

"Good," I said. "Because that's just what we're having for dinner. A medium-rare roast. Well, I've got to be getting back to school, Mr. Morgan. See you this evening."

He walked me to the door.

"Send your grandma my regards, will you?"

"Oh I will. And I know she'll be happy to get them. She's really been happy lately."

"I'm glad to hear that," he said. "She's a lovely woman and I enjoy her company."

"She enjoys yours too. She loves coming to the shop and being with you every day. And I just know that everything's going to work out okay."

Mr. Morgan looked puzzled. "I beg your pardon?"

"Well, you know," I began, and felt a little embarrassed.

"Go on, Sheila. I know what?"

"It's just that I've heard how hard it is for people on

social security to live. And I want you to know that if you and Bubbie ever decide to get married or something...Well, you shouldn't worry about having to live on a single meager check. Because I'm sure that Mother and Daddy will be glad to help out. Especially during the tax season."

Mr. Morgan was silent.

"Mr. Morgan, you okay?"

"What? Oh, yes, Sheila. Fine, just fine. But I guess you'd better be going now."

"I guess I'd better. See you this evening, Mr. Morgan."

When I got back from school I told my mother, "I saw Mr. Morgan before and he likes his meat medium-rare."

My mother's mouth fell open. "Oh, Sheila. You mean to tell me that you actually went to him and asked him?"

"Don't worry. I was tactful."

By dinnertime the medium-rare roast was ready. So was Bubbie, looking positively beautiful in her pale-blue dress. I hoped Mr. Morgan wouldn't forget the rose. Daddy took off work special again and Muriel had a late date with Ralph. So we were all there together, waiting for Mr. Morgan to come to dinner. We waited and waited. Bubbie sat at the table with her hands in her lap.

"The roast is drying out," said Mother.

We waited some more. But Julius Morgan never showed.

"What do you think happened to him?" I asked Muriel the next day. Bubbie had gone to see Mr. Morgan because she was worried about him, and we were waiting for her to come back. She tried to call him the night before but couldn't find his name in the phone book or from Information.

"Maybe he had a big business deal," said Muriel. "Like a chance to buy a rare antique. Or maybe he just forgot."

"He couldn't have forgotten. That's all we talked about when I saw him yesterday."

After a while we heard the back door open, followed by slow, heavy footsteps on the stairs. Muriel and I ran into the kitchen and waited at the door. Bubbie walked in slowly and her face was white and pasty-looking like Mrs. Plumb's.

Mother glanced up from the book she was reading, and when she saw Bubbie she said, "Ma, what's wrong? What's the matter?"

Bubbie didn't answer. She stared straight ahead and spoke to the air around her. "Such a fool. I feel like such a fool."

Mother helped her to a chair. "Ma, come sit down. Tell me what happened. Did you see Mr. Morgan? Is he all right?"

Bubbie looked up at Mother, and I could see the

tears fill up in her eyes. "Such craziness. I never heard such craziness. The man tells me he doesn't want to get married. He's too old to start all over again. He's sorry I had the wrong idea. Can you imagine? He thinks I want to get married. How could he believe such a thing? What nonsense. I had to explain to him. It was the company...someone to be with...someone to talk to. It was somewhere to go...something to do every day. I could wake up in the morning and know that I would have something to do. He made me feel like such a fool." Then Bubbie got up and went to her room, and I burst out of the kitchen, crying.

I ran into the bathroom and slammed the door. I leaned against it and cried and cried, just thinking how I ruined Bubbie's life and how she'd probably want to go away to an Old People's Home so she wouldn't ever have to look at me again. The next thing I knew, Mother was banging on the door and yelling, "Sheila, what's going on? What's this all about? Open the door."

"No," I cried. "I'm never going to open it. I'm never coming out. I'm staying here for the rest of my life."

Then Muriel started on me. "Boy, Sheila. It sure sounds like you and Mr. Morgan had lots to talk about when you saw him yesterday."

"Shut up, Muriel. Go away and leave me alone."

"That might be a good idea," I heard Mother say. "Let's go. She'll come out when she's ready."

Ready? I'll never be ready, I told myself. And I went to the bathroom so I could cry some more. Then when I was all cried out, I got up and walked out of the bathroom.

I was exhausted. Exhausted and miserable. I needed a place to lie down and I needed to be alone. Muriel was in the living room practicing her stupid "Happy Farmer" and Mother was in my room, probably learning how I messed up Bubbie's life.

There was nowhere to go except Muriel's room. I walked into her bedroom and let myself fall into her bed. It felt good to be lying down. For a while I just lay there, tracing the circles and squares on Muriel's quilt. And then my hand reached under her pillow and pulled out the journal.

10:00 p.m.   Ralph. Ralph is wonderful. He has wonderful brown eyes and wonderful brown hair and a wonderful smile. Ralph is romantic. Even though he doesn't know it. He brought me a single red rose. I love red roses. I love Ralph. I'm in love with Ralph. Is loving and being in love the same thing? If not, what's the difference? I'll ask Elaine. She'll know. She's been in love lots of times. Ralph. Does Ralph love me? I don't know because he hasn't said so. But I think he does, by the way he looks at me, and the way he always holds my hand. He's kissed me 3 times so far. Once on the cheek and twice for real—on the mouth. Like on TV. At first I was afraid I wouldn't know how to do it. But it came naturally. It felt very warm and very good. That's how I feel inside too. Warm and good.

There was more on the next page, but I didn't go on. I just couldn't. What was happening to me? Reading Muriel's journal should have made me feel better, but this time I felt even worse. Before when I read the journal, I was just reading a lot of words that Muriel had written. But now it was as if I was going right inside her. Into her head—and into her heart too. And I knew I had no right being there. Mr. Morgan was none of my business either. I closed it up and slipped it back under her pillow — forever.

I heard Mother leave the bedroom. I waited a few minutes and then I went in to see Bubbie. I knew I'd have to see her sooner or later to tell her how sorry I was for messing things up for her.

She was sitting in her chair, looking out the window. She turned toward me when she heard the door open.

"Bubbie?"

She held her arms out to me and I ran to her. "Oh, Bubbie. I'm so sorry. I didn't mean for things to turn out this way."

She held me in her arms and rocked me, and I cried again, and the tears spilled out all over her flowered house dress.

Bubbie stroked my hair and said, "Sh, Sheila. It's all right. There's nothing to be sorry for."

"But it's all my fault that you don't have Mr. Morgan as a friend anymore."

"A friend? How much of a friend was he? Not a word, not a phone call. He just didn't come. He didn't care enough to come and ask me if what you said was true. He believed only what he wanted to. And when I tried to explain things to him he didn't care enough to listen. No, Sheila. There was nothing to spoil." Then Bubbie smiled at me and said, "I was getting tired of his cooking anyway."

I sat on her lap and we looked out the window, watching the last of winter melt away. "I've given up reading Muriel's journal," I told her.

"I'm glad you did, Sheila. And I knew you would too, sooner or later."

"Really? How?"

"Oh, I don't know. It was just a feeling I had."

"But I'll miss her journal. I won't have anything to read anymore."

"Did you ever think of writing your own journal?"

"What would I write about? I wouldn't know what to say."

"I think you must have all kinds of good thoughts and feelings locked up inside you. And if you start writing, everything will come pouring out. You'll see."

"My handwriting isn't very good."

"So who would know?"

"That's right. No one would. Because *my* journal would really be private. I wouldn't just stick it under my pillow where anyone could get at it. I would find a very private place where no one would ever look."

"I just know you'll find a very good place," Bubbie said, and she smiled and gave me a quick hug.

During the next few days Bubbie stayed in her room a lot and moped around the house. Mother had lots of talks with her. Daddy had talks with her too, whenever he was home long enough and didn't have his face stuck in one of his electronic calculators. And sometimes the three of them had talks together over coffee and kaiser rolls.

Then on the first day of April there was a phone call from Uncle Alex in Lakewood. Uncle Alex is Mother's youngest brother, and I love it when he calls so I can say hello to him and the rest of the family.

Everyone but me was in the kitchen when the call came. I was in the bathroom, getting ready to try on some of Muriel's lip gloss. But as soon as I realized who Mother was talking to I started for the kitchen. Something I heard made me stop short.

"...hasn't worked out. She wants to leave. Yes, maybe it's best for her. We're sorry...it's Ma's decision. Here, I'll let you talk to her."

I didn't want to hear any more. Bubbie was leaving!

She was going off to an Old People's Home after all, and I didn't want to hear about it.

I ran to my room and shut the door. How could she want to leave? How could an Old People's Home be better than here? I couldn't believe it.

I leaned against the door and heard Mother's words all over again. It hasn't worked out. She wants to leave. And then I knew there was only one thing left for me to do.

Eleven

I would run away from home. There was nothing left to stay for. Because of me Bubbie was going to an Old People's Home, and I just couldn't stick around anymore.

I brought up a small suitcase from the basement and opened it up on my bed. I threw in a pair of jeans and some socks and underwear.

It wasn't just my fault that Bubbie was leaving. It was Mother's fault too. She never gave Bubbie enough to do around the house. Before Mr. Morgan, all Bubbie ever did was sit around in her chair all day.

I threw in a hairbrush.

If that's all an old person can do, then I don't ever want to get old. I'd rather die than have to sit around in a chair all day.

I threw in my toothbrush and a tube of toothpaste.

Mother never even gave Bubbie a doll talk or a picture talk. She was too busy giving them to other people. And now they were letting her go away.

I found some loose change in my junk drawer and stuck it in my pocket.

Well, if Bubbie was going, I was going too. I was all set and ready to leave, so I took one last look around my room. I don't ever remember it looking so pretty. Good-bye, room. Good-bye, everyone. Good-bye, Bubbie. I'll miss you, but this is the only way. I'll leave you my Purple Passion to remember me by.

I picked up the suitcase, took a few more last looks around, and sneaked out the front door. I didn't even bother to leave a note.

Where do people go when they run away? I didn't know. I thought of taking a bus ride until the end of the line. But where would I go from there? Well, I couldn't just stand in the middle of the street thinking about it, so I went over to Rita's. Maybe she would have some ideas.

I rang the bell and Rita opened the door. She was eating a chocolate cupcake.

"Hi, Sheila. Where are you going with the suitcase? Camp doesn't start until the end of June."

"I'm running away from home."

"Ha, ha, April Fool!" Rita shrieked, almost choking on the crumbs. "Oh, Sheila, you're a riot."

"I am not a riot. And this is not a joke. I'm really running away."

"Now, Sheila, don't do anything you'll be sorry for. Let's sit down and talk this thing over."

I put the suitcase on the sidewalk and sat down on the steps to tell her why I had to run away. "... And now my grandma and Mr. Morgan won't get married and my grandma is going away to an Old People's Home and everything is all my fault."

"Gee, that's too bad, Sheila. But don't you see what you have to do?"

"Sure I see. And I'm doing it. I'm leaving."

"Wrong. You're going back home. Now. You're going to talk your grandmother out of going away. You're going to talk your folks out of letting her go."

"I won't be able to do anything."

"You've got to at least try. You can't just let it all happen without trying. Go home, Sheila. Go home and try."

When I walked in through the kitchen door Mother asked, "Where were you going with the suitcase, Sheila? We've been looking all over for you."

"I was playing an April Fool's joke on Rita," I said, and I went to my room to unpack.

A few minutes later my mother came in and sat next to me on the bed.

"Where were you going, Sheila? Really?"

"I don't know. Just away. Anywhere. I didn't want to stick around and watch Bubbie leave."

"So," Mother sighed, "you know about that."

"I heard you talking to Uncle Alex."

"Oh, Sheila, I'm so sorry you had to find out that way. I wish you hadn't left so we could have explained things to you."

"What's there to explain? Bubbie's leaving and it's my fault she's going."

"Your fault?" Mother said, and put her arms around me. "Sheila, of course it's not your fault. Nobody's blaming you for what's happened. And you shouldn't blame yourself either. I've spoken with Bubbie several times and she told me that she thought of leaving long ago. Things just haven't been right for her since she came here. And she hasn't really been happy. So I guess if anyone's to blame, it's me."

"It's just that she doesn't have enough to do around the house. You never let her do all the things she likes to do."

"It might seem that way to you, Sheila, and maybe you're right. But when it comes to those we love, it's not always easy to know what to do. We want so much to be good to them that we sometimes end up being *too* good. And maybe that's how I've been with Bubbie. But I want you to know, whatever I might have done, whatever I might have said, it's because I love her."

"Then maybe it's not too late," I said. And I felt so full of hope that I might be able to fix it so Bubbie wouldn't go away. "You can tell Bubbie that everything will be different now. And that from now on she can do anything she wants. And then you can give her all kinds of jobs to keep her busy. Maybe then she won't have to go away to the Old People's Home."

Mother got up from the bed. "The Old People's Home? Why, Sheila, what on earth ever gave you that idea?"

"Well, that's what we're talking about, isn't it? You said so yourself. It hasn't worked out. She's not happy here. She's going away...."

"Going away, yes. But not to an Old People's Home. She's going to live with Uncle Alex and his family in Lakewood."

"In Lakewood? You mean she's not going to an Old Home?"

Mother shook her head. "Of course not."

I felt a little better. After all, Lakewood and the chicken farm was better than an Old People's Home. But why did Bubbie have to leave at all?

"Why does she have to go anywhere?" I asked. "Why can't she just stay here? With us? You can tell her about all those jobs you'll give her and how busy she'll be."

Mother shook her head again. "I don't know that I would do things any differently. I don't know that I could. I think it might be best to let Bubbie go and decide things on her own."

I went into the living room. Muriel was playing something on the piano. It wasn't "The Happy Farmer." I sat down next to her.

"It isn't fair," I said.

She stopped playing and looked at me. "We can't be selfish, Sheila. We've had Bubbie all our lives so far. Just think how lucky we've been. We have cousins who have barely had a chance to know her. It's their turn now."

I knew I shouldn't be selfish. But I was. And I didn't care. And I was jealous too. I wanted Bubbie to stay with me. I didn't want her spending time with my cousins, baking them Surprise cookies and teaching them how to make cuttings from Purple Passions.

After Muriel left I started to play my Bach minuet. But it didn't feel right. So I played something of my own. It was soft and low and it sounded sad. And my music made me feel sorry for myself. And I felt sorry for Bubbie because she was leaving and I felt sorry for Bach because he was poor.

Bubbie walked into the living room just as I was finished playing.

"I'm glad you're back," she said. "I was out looking for you. I wanted to talk to you...to tell you...but your mama says you already know."

"Then it's for sure, isn't it," I said, without looking up. "You're going away."

"Yes, Sheila dear."

"Bubbie," I said, and looked up from the piano, "Bubbie, will you tell me the truth? Are you leaving because of me and Mr. Morgan?"

Bubbie leaned over and grabbed my arms. "No, Sheila, no. You must never think that."

"Then why can't you stay?"

She straightened up and walked over to the window and looked out at the street.

"It's just time to go, that's all. It's time for a change. Time for something new."

"But I'll make things better for you if you stay. I promise."

Bubbie turned to me and motioned for me to come to her. I walked over and she put her arm around me.

"Sheila dear, you have always made things better for me. You know that, don't you?"

I nodded and we looked out of the window together.

It rained in the night. A crash of thunder woke me and I sat up in bed with the covers over my head. In the darkness I could hear the sound of Bubbie snoring in time to the raindrops beating against the windows, and suddenly I wasn't afraid anymore. I tried to picture what it would be like when she was gone, the bed empty, without her. And I became afraid all over again.

Daddy came into the room, the way he always does during a storm. "Sheila," he said quietly.

"I'm afraid, Daddy."

He sat next to me and cradled my head in his arms. "The thunder can't hurt you," he whispered.

"I'm not afraid of the thunder. I'm afraid for Bubbie. She's old, Daddy. Eighty years old."

"She's only seventy-nine, remember? And that's not

so very old if you think about it. Abraham lived for a hundred and seventy-five years, and his wife Sarah lived to be a hundred and twenty-seven. Now, *that's* old."

"Oh, Daddy, please don't ever get old." I snuggled up closer to him. "It must be awful to be old."

"It's not awful to be old. As long as you feel wanted ... and needed. It's the loneliness that's awful. But loneliness can be awful at any age."

"Bubbie *is* wanted and needed. Isn't she?"

"You bet she is. So go to sleep now, baby, and don't you worry about Bubbie. She'll get along just fine." He kissed my forehead and sat with me for a little while. After he left I pulled the covers back over my head and went to sleep.

By morning the rain had stopped. I helped Bubbie make the beds. Then I sat with her at the table watching her eat her soggy kaiser roll and thinking how I might never see her dunk another roll again.

"When will you be leaving?" I asked her.

"Not right away. Maybe in a couple of weeks. We still have plenty of time together."

When breakfast was over Bubbie looked out of the window and said, "Such a pretty day. It's a shame to waste such a day. Sheila dear, come. We'll go for a walk. A nice long walk."

Mother started to say something but stopped suddenly and turned away.

We went out into the street. The pavement was wet and shiny, with little colored circles all around. "Look," I said, "there are rainbows in the street."

"And spring is in the air," Bubbie said. "Can you smell it, Sheila?"

"I don't want spring to be here," I told her. "Spring means you're going away, and I want you to stay here." We stepped down a steep curb and I took her arm.

"Will you ever come back?"

"To visit—of course. To live—maybe. Who knows? A person never can tell about certain things."

"I hope you come back, Bubbie. Otherwise I'll miss you. Even more than I missed the Saturday walks to your house and Myron and the Eskimo Pies. If you live in Lakewood, I just know I'll never get to see you."

"Certainly you'll see me. You'll come to visit me too. Every summer you'll come and help me on the farm. And in between summers I'll have my thoughts of you, and my pictures, and the nice new album that you got for me."

"And you'll have your chair," I reminded her.

"No, not the chair. That I'll leave here — for you. You'll find that it holds a wonderful secret."

"Really?" I squealed. "What kind of secret?"

"If I tell you, it won't be a secret. But you'll find it yourself, if you look hard enough."

I wished I could fly right home and find out what

could be secret about her chair, but Bubbie seemed anxious to finish her walk. So arm in arm we walked slowly down the street, past the old lady's fish store and J. Morgan Antiques. Bubbie gave a quick glance at the shop and turned away. We walked on until we came to Forty Fantastic Flavors. I stopped to look at the posters in the windows advertising all the new flavors. Nutty Navel Orange. I'd have to try that one next.

Ahead of us was the drugstore. When we got there Bubbie said she wanted to go in to get something. I started to go in with her, but she stopped me. "No, let me go in alone."

Well, that was okay. Maybe she wanted to buy something private and didn't want me to see. Maybe she needed some more Efferdent. So she went in and I waited. And when she came out she was carrying a large brown bag. "It's part of the secret too," she said.

It's bedtime now. And I'm sitting in Bubbie's chair pretending that I'm a hundred and twenty-seven years old — like Sarah — and that those are my teeth sitting there in that glass on the window sill. One of these days before Bubbie leaves for Lakewood, I'm going to walk right up to those teeth and look them straight in the gums — just to prove to myself that I can do it.

The Purple Passions are still on the window sills too. I'm giving mine to Bubbie and she's giving me all of

hers. She said that they'll help me to remember her.
if I could ever forget her.

already found out the chair's secret, even
took me a whole day to figure it out. The
chair aren't just ordinary thick, ugly old
y're very special thick, ugly old arms. The
panels on top of each arm slide back to reveal
most wonderful hiding places deep inside. And
hat's not all. When I looked in the hiding places, I saw
that one arm was empty. But in the other one there
was a brand-new blue spiral notebook. It isn't just an
ordinary blue spiral notebook either, because on the
cover, written in pencil, in a shaky handwriting, is
SHEILA'S JOURNAL. So I guess I'll write my journal
after all. It'll be very private and *very* creative. And
I'll hide it in the chair where no one will ever look. Not
even Bubbie, I know, because she gave that hiding
place to me.

Maybe I'll even write about Bubbie. That way I can
keep her with me even when she's gone. Yes, that's
what I think I'll do. At least that's a good place to
start.